KERA FAIRE

EVERNIGHT PUBLISHING ®

www.evernightpublishing.com

Copyright© 2017

Kera Faire

Editor: JS Cook

Cover Artist: Jay Aheer

ISBN: 978-1-77339-277-6

KERA FAIRE

DEDICATION

To Lindsey. I hope you like your story.

Thanks to you and all at one specific glass works for your help and information, and giving me the chance to see how glass is made. Any mistakes are mine.

KERA FAIRE

THE FURNACE MAN

Death Isle, 5

Kera Faire

Copyright © 2017

Prologue

"So tell me husband *dearest,*" the voice was laced with sarcasm, "just what does my darling other half do, that means when I try to contact him his phone goes to voicemail every bloody time? How can a director of a whisky company be unavailable every minute of the day *and* night?" She was working up a fine head of steam and Michael could imagine he could see smoke coming out of her ears. Lord, how he loved his feisty lady.
Nevertheless, it would have been easier to deal with sulks and tantrums. Not this icy cold contempt, which was about to turn to red-hot but not explosive. That wasn't his lady's way.

Even so, she looked ready to murder someone. Or cut their balls off, and he was right in the firing line. Petite and slim but with curves in all the right places, her blonde hair was all over the place as she poked him in the chest with one non-bitten red-tipped nail. Fuck-me-red varnish and perfectly manicured. *Bloody hell.* His cock hardened to a painful rod and his balls stiffened with anticipation.

Poor sods, he thought. There wasn't a cat in hell's

chance any of that particular area of his body was going to get the relief it wanted. Unless his own hands got busy, and the likelihood of that, at that moment in time, was a big fat 'not a scooby'.

"Since when did you not bite your nails?" he asked with interest. He'd never known her without ragged nails, which she had always been at pains to hide. These perfectly shaped talons were definitely cum-inducing. "Looking good, pet. I like the varnish."

"Good for you," Lindsey retorted. "Zero out of ten for observation. I haven't bitten them in over a year, and I've had them professionally done for at least ten months. But, oh yeah, I forgot, you wouldn't know that. After all, you're never here to notice, are you? Oh and silly me. On the odd occasion you do turn up, well, why look at my hands when all you're interested in is my pussy? Fuck me, and flop. Well fuck me, no more fucking me is on the cards, mate. Not till you 'fess up." She took a deep breath followed by what sounded suspiciously like a sob. "Who is she?"

He stared at her blankly. What was she talking about? He smothered a yawn. Lord, he was so bloody knackered all he wanted was sleep. Then to make love to his wife, sate himself in her. Play a little and try his new nipple clamps out on her luscious tits. Ha, and that, he reckoned with a sinking feeling, was as likely as flying pigs. Why oh why was his working life so incompatible with his home life? Why did he have the tingle that informed him love was not enough? Now it seemed his wife thought he had someone else in his life. Surely not as…?

"She?" Michael asked warily. "She, who?" It couldn't be his boss. He was a guy. Someone who he was damned sure wasn't on Lindsey's radar. There was no one else, unless…*Oh fuck.*

"Whoever you're screwing," Lindsey said impatiently. "'Cos it sure as hell ain't me."

"I'm not screwing anyone," he protested, well aware how pathetic he sounded. "I love you, Lins, you know that."

"Do I?" She raised both eyebrows, her unusual blue-green eyes cloudy, her lashes dark against her pale skin. It was one of life's mysteries why her hair—everywhere except her lashes—was blonde.

Her expression was reflective and somber, and a splash of color over her high cheekbones was the only brightness he could detect. And that, he knew, was from temper.

"I wonder, Michael, I really do. I love you, I thought I knew you, and I sure as hell believed in 'til death us do part. Now though? If you're not playing around and dipping your wick elsewhere, what the fuck is going on?"

Fuck? From Lindsey, who never swore? Fuck several times *and* pussy in less than a minute. Hell, he was deep in the shit. And sadly, he could say nothing to defend himself. As for playing? *What the*... Just before he made an even bigger mess of everything, Michael realized she didn't mean their sort of playing.

"Cat got your tongue?" Lindsey demanded harshly. "Oh no I forgot: we don't have a cat. A cat needs looking after and you, I quote 'didn't think it fair as you were away so often'. Must be nice to think about things like that. Maybe you should have had the same thoughts about a wife."

He winced. She didn't notice, as she was so caught up in her ire.

"You know." She poked him again. Those talons were sharp. Michael was glad of his t-shirt.

"Look, Lins…" he began. He didn't get a chance

to say what he wanted her to look at before she narrowed her eyes, glared—she had a good line in glares—and broke in.

"Nope. You look," she commanded. "Think on this. Ask yourself something. Go on, say to yourself, 'is it fair to have a wife when I'm away so often?' You said it enough when I asked for a dog. Even though I was around and with more than a little spare time on my hands, your argument was that you—*you* mind you—wouldn't be able to give it the attention it deserved. A wife, though? You obviously don't give her the same courtesy. Which is shite. Because you know, it's as bad neglecting a human as an animal. Something you do, all the time." She held her hand up to stop him voicing an opinion. "Let me finish."

After her previous knock back, he actually hadn't intended to add anything. How could he when sadly, everything she said was true?

"And another thing, how come if I phone your office the call is diverted?" Lindsey went on, oblivious—luckily—to his rigid stance. "How come for that matter you allegedly work from home a lot as well, but you're never here? That you have two passports and I only ever see one? How come...*oooft*!" Lindsey glared at him as he shut her up most effectively by covering her mouth with his hand. Enough was enough. He waited for her to bite him.

Her eyes widened and the angry glint went out of them. Instead she looked defeated. Sad, resigned and reconciled with something he decided he wasn't going to like.

"I tell you what I can," he said quietly. Even that was too much to say, but sod it, this was his wife. His wife, his life and if he wasn't mistaken, his marriage at stake. Was the bloody job worth it? "And I shouldn't even say that. Hell, Lindsey, I love you. I wouldn't cheat on you. Never ever." It had never even crossed his mind. She was all he wanted.

Lindsey sighed and her breath tickled his palm. Michael lifted his hand with care as she smiled with such a sad expression on her face he could have cried. That weary, haunted look of despair was all his fault.

"I accept that you're not cheating on me with a woman." She half laughed. "Or a bloke, for that matter, but it's not going to change, is it? You are cheating me out of something. Whatever it is you do, and please grant me the intelligence to know it's not just all whisky related, you're not going to share it with me. That's cheating in my book."

He shrugged as if his heart wasn't splintering into tiny little bits that bombarded him with pain. The sort of pain he didn't know was possible to receive and still stay upright. "I can't tell you anything. There's nothing to tell."

She shook her head and bit her lip. Her face was white, her expression resolute. "Really?" she said. "I'm sorry to be a skeptic, Michael. More sorry than you'll ever know, but I can't stay in a marriage where one of the partners isn't open and honest," she added, sadder than he'd ever seen her. "I accept you're not playing away, but you're doing something you're not sharing with me. I can't live like that, always wondering, never sure. Hell, you might be a spy or a bloody drug dealer, for all I know about it."

Little did she realize. "I despise drugs and anyone who has anything to do with them."

"So you're a spy." She laughed and thankfully didn't look at him. "That'll be right. So Mr. Bond, go and make someone else's life hell. I'm there already."

He had a nasty suspicion he was about to join her,

but he had to make one last plea for another chance.

"Lin…oh shit." His phone blared out its insistent 'answer me now' noise. "I'd better take this." It had to be his proper boss. He recognized the tone.

"Yeah oh shit," she mimicked. "Story of our life, eh? Your phone rings and you disappear. Well hey, I'll save you the need to think up a reason why a director of a whisky company has to go to Bora Bora or Tierra Del Fuego or wherever. I'll go first, and not to there. Where I go will be up to me. And no, I won't bother to tell you where or why either." She stood on tiptoe and kissed his three-day-old stubble. "I could say so long, it's been good to know you." She swallowed and the noise was like a death knell to him. "But I'm not sure at the moment if that is true or not."

Michael watched, silent and unmoving as she took one step back, then another, before she turned around. Her eyes glistened with tears and two red spots showed on her otherwise ashen cheeks.

"I did love you," she said softly. "But it wasn't enough, was it?"

Don't go. But he didn't say it aloud. What right had he to beg her to stay? In a marriage where he was away more than he was home, and he told more lies than truths.

Chapter One

"Pet, you need to listen carefully." The hand on her ass was hard, stinging, and she welcomed the pain. "I'm going to fuck you deep and fast. From behind, and enjoy watching those luscious red cheeks move for me. Five more on each side I think, to make them glow. Count for me pet. Color?"

"Green, oh god, ahhh…" The spanks rained down on her bottom and she arched into them, embracing the sensation of being wanted by her Sir.

Lindsey moaned and counted the strikes. By the tenth she was floating. As he entered her, and his balls slapped against her she pushed back, to help him get even further inside her. To connect with him. To be his pet. His sub. His. Only his.

Her boobs swayed and he reached around and pinched one nipple hard.

"Next time I'm putting clamps and a chain on. Watch your tits sway and feel you come alive to that pain." His breath grew harsh as she watched him, panting with each thrust. The pictures he conjured up gathered her juices and made her even more wet and needy.

He stiffened, and she groaned.

"Now pet, come for me … now." He roared the words, bent so his chest hair rasped across her back and before she could beg for more, he bit her neck.

Hot cum filled her as he shouted out his completion.

Her climax overwhelmed her and she screamed. "Michael!"

The name echoed around her mind.

Lindsey writhed in the bed. The empty except for her bed.

Outside, the early predawn showed it wasn't time to get up. Inside, the sheets were twisted around her legs and her hair was plastered to her face. She swore and pushed the damp strands back with shaking hands.

That bloody dream again. She glanced at the clock. Plenty of time.

Now where the hell was her bullet?

****

Whoever said the life of a spy was exciting, hadn't worked *her* job.

It was more exciting watching two snails race—s...l...o...w...l...y...—or the way her ex 'mark two' fucked and that on a scale of one to ten rated a big fat zero—than this. The expression, 'check the size of a guy's finger to determine the size of his cock' was correct. He had a finger the size of a gherkin, and a cock to match.

Now Michael... No, do not go there. Just, she admonished herself, do not. If that hadn't been such a monumental mistake, maybe she wouldn't have jumped into that stupid, but luckily very short-lived, relationship with an asshole. Men were secretive, manipulative assholes. And overeager pricks. She should have learned from her marriage, to whom she thought was going to be the love of her life forever, not to jump into anything without a lot of thought.

Not the best of track records.

Mind you, it was that stupidity that brought her into her present line of work. A boring dead-end job, originally taken so she was around on the off chance 'he' might be there with her, the interlude with the asshole latest ex and a short advert in *The Times*. Six rounds of interviews and tests later, she found herself signing the Official Secrets Act and undertaking several months of intensive training. And for what?

Boredom. Unrelieved, unadulterated boredom. She'd have been better off staying where she was. At least she wouldn't be here, in the one part of the country she'd been glad to leave. After uni she'd been happy to spread her wings. Never did she expect all these years later to be back not ten miles from where she'd started.

Bored rigid.

Truth to say she had never been so stultified in her life and she was the sort of person who usually found something interesting in everything she did.

Usually.

"Hey love, that's me off. See you whenever. Don't forget we've got new starts tomorrow. Can you rustle up some starter forms? I forgot earlier."

Lindsey jumped as the cheerful voice interrupted her introspection and brought her mind back to the there and then. "Sure." It would pass ten minutes. Lindsey smiled at Jinnie, the departing early evening shift receptionist and wished it were her who was going home instead. There was a good book and a hot bath with her name on them waiting there. Instead she had eight long hours at the coalface—or in this case the Glassworks— before she could swan out with a casual wave.

Hello, and welcome to another night of boredom and thumb twiddling. Where no one tries to fling a body into the furnace and I repaint my nails for the eighth time in a week. At least she *was* varnishing her own these days and not reliant on a professional job. It helped to pass the time.

Jinnie, who let the door bang behind her, with a cheerful "see ya," was lucky enough to work when some people were around. She had 'proper' typing to do and allegedly important phone calls to answer during her shift. Lindsey couldn't confirm or deny that, as all she ever got during her hours on reception was to type up the canteen menu and tell cranks and pervs to fuck off. Nothing else.

No deliveries, no visitors. Bugger all except the less than imaginative weirdoes on the end of the phone line, with nothing better to do than jerk off as they talked to her.

It felt like she had read more books in the time she'd been there than in the rest of her life, crocheted three hats and a scarf and knitted three cushion covers. And still had time to swivel in her chair, stave off sleep with coffee and chocolate and slam the phone down on the deviants.

Sadly, her usual response to those callers might need changing now, after the last bloke had said 'yes please' and rang back three times to tell her how he was going to do it.

Eugh. The thought of him made her skin crawl. She'd spent several early mornings walking across the car park to get to her car with her keys held ready to gouge out the eyes of anyone she didn't know, if they approached her. Nobody came anywhere near but she was even more careful what she said and did nowadays. Her boss, her real boss, not Gary, the bossman at the Glassworks—an appropriate name for a glassworks she thought, if somewhat predictable—had warned her to be vigilant and boy, she intended to do as he commanded. Sometimes when she listened to his voice she wondered about him.

Darke, not Gary.

By name and by nature she surmised. And wouldn't be surprised if there wasn't a hint of the dominant in him. Every word he spoke, the timbre of his voice hinted of it. A man used to being obeyed in every facet of his life.

As the department had directed, she had to go

through the motions, note down anything untoward—nothing yet in the three weeks she'd been there unless you counted the other perv who wanted her to tell him he was a good boy changing his tune, and asking her to tell him he was very naughty and detail what she wanted him to do to make amends. 'Fuck off' didn't work there either. She'd just blown a police whistle down the phone. He hadn't rung since. Other than that, zilch. Even the sparrows cleared off and left the trees empty once it got dark.

Is this my life? Looking for someone who might, just might, mind you—they had no real evidence as yet—be using the company to get rid of persons unspecified for reasons unknown. Who, why, where, no one knew. But they all—her included—hoped somehow she'd find out and not become one of those missing in the process.

Lindsey draped her jacket over the back of the chair before she adjusted the seat to her height. Jinnie was tall and built like a Rubens portrait. Lindsey wasn't. Not that it bothered her. She was happy and comfortable in her own skin.

What she wasn't happy and comfortable about was having to be there at the Glassworks. After all, it wasn't even her night to work. She'd earmarked a large gin and tonic, a bath and a book—with a particularly hot and horny hero—for the evening, followed by an early bed. Instead here she was, no gin, no book, no bed, and no hero.

A late phone call from Gary the bossman had asked her to cover for Katrina, the usual girl, who had fallen off her horse and broken her ankle that afternoon. As Lindsey had taken several days off the previous week with 'flu', a euphemism for having to go and meet her true boss for a catch up and a briefing, she couldn't complain. After all, if nothing ever untoward happened on her rostered nights at the factory, maybe tonight she would strike lucky?

Deep in thought, Lindsey made a pot of strong coffee, grimaced at the taste and wondered why it was so vile. Anyone would think it had dead bodies in it.

Argh no, not dead bodies. She nipped into the ladies and flushed the rest of the pigswill down the sink. Surely coffee beans didn't go off from one day to the next? If she hadn't seen it was the same packet she'd used for several nights, she would've said someone had swapped the granules for some ground three years before, instead of a mere three days.

However it was an undisputed fact whenever they'd been ground, they tasted awful. She'd stick to the bottled water she brought from home. Surely the coffee wasn't usually that bad? Bitter and sickly and it made her feel nauseous. She'd only had a few sips, and she dreaded to think how she would have felt if she'd finished it all.

Bored already—Lindsey wasn't someone who could be idle without a book in her hand—she stared through the large window into the darkened yard beyond. One lone security light lit up the empty space directly outside, creating shifting shapes in the shadows that led to the bright-as-day furnace building. Inside there was a full shift of workers creating whatever bottles were needed, but elsewhere was a different story.

It was creepy. Enough to make you wonder what hid behind a corner. She laughed at her fanciful thoughts. Hell, the inaction was getting to her brain. How on earth did people stand pretending to be busy in a job where they actually did very little?

As ever, the diary said there were no deliveries due that night. Tomorrow they had sand coming but as ever nothing arrived after six. So, damn it, she would have to resort to counting the squashed bugs on the window yet again. Why did the Glassworks need a three-shift reception anyway? Oh it was handy for her department—her real employers—that was for sure, as it gave them an operative in place, but lord it was stultifying. Worse than watching paint dry. Surely they didn't need anybody there at night? It wasn't as if reps or potential customers would just drop in at midnight on the off chance someone was around to answer their question about whether they could look forward to a new order, or were getting the big heave ho? Couldn't they just lock up and leave the gateman in charge? He'd have to open the gates to let anyone in, so surely it was as easy to turn people away?

Okay, the place worked 24/7 and there were plenty of people about if you knew where to look for them, but in the office block? Her and a few mice. Not another body to be seen.

A body? Oh hell. That of course was why she was there. *Shit, do not think of a body. A person. Me, a totally live—well almost—I can't make any promises about all of my body being alive—person.* She mentally rolled her eyes at her thoughts. When was the last time she used all of said body in a myriad of ways? Specifically her pussy? Too long ago to remember. Even the hot as hell guy who had done his best to pick her up and seduce her just before she'd started her job hadn't touched her. Not after she threatened to cut off his balls with a rusty pen knife if he didn't give over and stop with the fake charm. She swore she saw a glimmer of appreciation before he did the oh so overdone hurt, 'I want you for you, I'm so not like that' shite. She hadn't been convinced, and sent him packing. It was still a source of amazement he'd gone without an argument.

Plus, if she didn't do the check your boobs thing regularly they would think they were redundant, it had been so long since any other hands touched them. Years…she just had no idea…

Rubbish, isn't. Don't lie. The last occasion was etched on her brain. As well as the time, date and fuck buddy. And what a shitty idea that had been. Oh the sex was amazing; there was no doubt about that. Her clit still tingled when she thought about it. Hell she could come without using Roger the rabbit when she thought of that guy and the way his green eyes lit up as he stroked her skin, played with her hair and whispered her name. *My Lindsey.*

My Lindsey. Load of rubbish. Enough already. Michael Coulter, ex number one, was out of her orbit. One night of bliss, an oh so romantic ceremony on the beach, followed by a shitty marriage, and sadly now she had the paper to prove it was over and done with. The big heave ho should now be history. She had to pull up her big girl knickers and get over him.

Pity she preferred thongs.

Chapter Two

The phone rang and she jumped. Hot coffee splashed over her hands and Lindsey swore as the pain hit her like a sadist's whip. She might like the sting but not in that way.

The message was short, sharp and succinct. Not totally unexpected, even if at times she thought it would *never* arrive, it warned her to beware. Something was amiss and no one knew exactly what. Not even if it meant something was going to happen near her. All she gleaned was that another operative, no name, no idea whom or where, had sent in an amber alert from the area. As 'the area' covered most of Yorkshire it could be a drugs drop in Scarborough or an illicit film in Ripon for all she knew. Miles and miles away. Sod it. Typical, because she'd brought a new and much anticipated BDSM book with her to read and had been looking forward to getting down and dirty—metaphorically speaking—with the sexy Dom hero. Instead she was going to have to be on guard. And to make matters worse, soon be aware and even more alert and not know to whom, or where.

Why was life never simple? Why out of every gin joint—okay every factory, furnace or flaming workplace did she draw the short straw and end up here? She sighed. It was her job. Her desire to do some good somehow. And she had to do her part in stopping the rot.

Lindsey waved to the guy on the gate who stood outside his little hut and stared at her for long enough to make her twitchy, before he waved back, and disappeared into his hut again. She returned to the reception desk and pulled up the daily info sheet on the computer. Somehow she'd missed the list of new starts when she'd slung her bag in the drawer and made the coffee, but she'd best get on and type it. If she only used one finger she could make it last oh, five minutes.

One name made her almost spill her coffee.

God almighty, what had she done to deserve that? She shut her eyes briefly and hoped she'd dreamed it.

She hadn't. There it was in bold black letters on the screen in front of her.

Derek Unwin Terence Turner. AKA Dutt.

Dutt. Surely not her ex? But a quick perusal of everything about him made her fairly certain.

Bloody Dutt the Fuck. Starting tomorrow. And bugger it, wouldn't you know she was working then as well. Of all the shite and rot that could float to the surface, that was the worst.

It was a pity the rot and her had a history, but that she guessed, was life rearing up and biting her in the bum.

Rot known as Dutt. Tall, dark—swarthy—and a manipulative bastard. She'd got away from his bullying clutches long ago, with a massive blow to her self-esteem, and if she never had to face him again that would be too soon. To be told he was about to become night shift furnace man was shite. How soon before they told her to hand in her notice and get the hell out? Sod's law that it probably wasn't likely for a while now Dutt the Fuck was around. It stunk. Was he what the 'beware' message was all about? She'd put money on it. That would be so like Darke.

What was Dutt doing back round there anyway? The last thing she had heard was he lived on the Costa Del Thieves, all loved up with the ex-mistress of a bloke doing thirty to life for reinforcing a motorway bridge— but not with concrete. Now he was purported to be back in England? Life sucked donkey balls sometimes.

But at least she was forewarned, forearmed, and

several years older, even if not that much wiser. She had been made aware that one of the pitfalls of knowing an area was the risk of being sent there to work or be a sleeper, but naively thought that as it was so long since she'd been resident in that part of Yorkshire, it wouldn't happen to her.

How wrong could a person be? Here she was with fucking Dutt about to be in her orbit again. Of course Darke arranged it. He was the king of manipulators.

What next? All she needed was for Michael Coulter to turn up as the new night gateman and she'd be a candidate for the local psychiatric hospital.

Oh no, she wasn't having that. One thing she did know was Dutt didn't have the power to manipulate her anymore and Michael didn't want to try.

Absently, Lindsey scanned the lists of what was being made that week, noticed one line was making black bottles and that the deliveries the next day—sadly not when she was there—was to be a delivery of frit—the dye to color the glass, along with a load of silica sand. It would have been interesting to see it. When she had her orientation, Lindsey had been fascinated by the process, especially watching the bottles being made. To be honest she had a hard time imagining just how they could *get* any bodies into the furnace to burn as her department suspected.

Every delivery was monitored and there was always staff around. Oh she accepted the somewhat macabre joke of 'don't piss off the furnace man or he'll burn you and you'll never be seen again except as a bottle' could be true, but surely a body couldn't just be disposed of like that? Anyone could see it for a start, and it was hardly likely the whole bloody night shift were assassins or assassins' mates.

Not only that, she was a bit hazy about the details,

but hadn't she heard somewhere tiny bits of the body might appear? Undertakers said thigh bones and stuff could sometimes stay intact. Wasn't teeth enamel the one thing you couldn't dispose of? Or was that only when pigs ate the bodies? She should have listened more when she'd had her 'methods of disposing of bodies 101' class.

Whatever the ins and outs of it all, she still had Dutt to contend with and he was enough for her to research other ways of disposal. This time of assholes. That thought, of those tiny puckered holes disappearing down a waste disposal or something similar, made her chuckle and she went back to sending her received and understood email to her boss in a much better mood. After all, it might expedite her removal from the Glassworks to somewhere more congenial.

The phone rang, and she picked it up absently, only to put it down with a crash that made *her* wince, let alone the 'I want to eat you out and do naughty things with you' tosser on the other end.

God almighty, what next? Flying pigs eating people? Well as long as one was Dutt, and that last caller, that was okay.

A tap-tap-tap on the window made her flinch and screw her eyes up to try and see from the light of the reception into the dark of the grounds. Her heart jumped as a face pressed to the glass and she gave a shaky laugh as she recognized who it was. Lord, this inactivity was making her jittery, and it needed to stop. Jitters were not acceptable. The itch and the need to be aware was.

Outside the window, Bernie the night gateman tapped his wrist and made miming gestures of drinking coffee. She nodded and five minutes later he appeared, with what looked and smelled like a better cup of java than she could ever produce. It was even more surprising when she knew all he had was an electric ring and a kettle. Both, she'd discovered, against the rules, but who was to know? She wasn't telling, that was for sure. Especially when he kept her sanity with the regular drinks and she supplied the cakes.

Lindsey opened the door, handed over a muffin, and grasped the mug with 'furnace men are hot' inscribed on it. "Cheers, Bernie, I'm ready for that. You nearly scared the pa...er breath out of me." She'd nearly said pants. Bernie might be the wrong side of sixty but he always had a definite glint in his eye that stopped her bandying anything even slightly risqué with him.

"No worries pet, you get that down you. All of it mind, 'cos it's a long night." He stared at her intently and she blinked. "Bloody Katrina," he said explosively. "Nice girl like you. You shouldn't have to work extra on such short notice."

Eh? What a strange thing to say. Lindsey wondered if she should ask him what he meant. Maybe it was just as well she didn't get the chance.

"Ah, well, best go check what's what." When she looked at him again he was his normal affable self. "Lovely baker you are, pet."

She nodded, decided not to say the baker was a well-known department store or that calling someone pet had very different connotations to her, and wandered to sit back behind the desk. She might as well look professional and in charge, even if her Kindle was open behind the desktop. She sipped her coffee and cringed. Had Bernie just used some from a week or so ago? Evidently looks and aroma could be deceptive. It tasted as bad as the one she'd made. Another sip confirmed that and it went down the sink like the previous one. What the hell had got into everyone? Was it a bad moon, or someone had forgotten to wish the area good karma? Whatever, it couldn't be over too quickly for her. She couldn't cope with Dutt *and* crap coffee.

Half an hour with her book and she'd hunt out those forms. Then what? Several hours of not very much. She might even practice some yoga. Whatever else, she was *not* going to paint her nails again. Apart from the fact she was bored with that activity, it was costing her a fortune in nail varnish. Could she indent Darke for it? Extra expenses: Blood Red and Sexy Lady nail polishes, £20 per bottle.

Ha, that would be the day. Her book it would have to be. It was pity it didn't hold her interest. She thought the hero an idiot, and as much a Dom as a chocolate button, and the heroine too stupid to live. She deleted it from her Kindle and contemplated the list of books on the tablet.

Back to the drawing board. In this case an old, well-loved hot as hell D/s shifter story. That was better.

Content now, Lindsey settled down to enjoy an hour of uninterrupted bliss.

Oh, the best laid plans and all that guff.

Lindsey yawned and shook her head to try and clear it. Why the hell did her brain feel so bloody fuzzy?

Chapter Three

"So, we go in and you head everything up, got that, bud?" The voice was nasal, crackly, like a rusty nail on a blackboard and grated like nothing else the man who reluctantly had to listen to it had ever known. If the speaker hadn't been built like a shoddily made brick shithouse, Michael might have made some comment about it. What he'd give for the chance to tell the asshole that he understood the Queen's English, even if said asshole didn't a lot of the time, and he, Michael, wasn't an incipient flower. He hated bloody stupid nicknames. Bud. God almighty, he might as well call him petal. Or flower.

As long as it wasn't pet. That was for him to use on others. Specifically...

Do not go there.

Unless... but that was different.

"You know you can't shag 'er but no one would know if y'copped a feel," the asshole went on. "Fucking good set of tits on 'er, and as for 'er pussy..." The asshole sniggered. "Does everything needed and some."

Michael gritted his teeth. God almighty, the man was an out-and-out sex offender, that was for sure. To say nothing of what else they suspected him of.

"Gotta love our Katrina. She's very obliging." Dutt winked. "Very. If you get my meaning."

"Yeah," Michael said laconically. No way were they going to try and pin that onto him. It was bad enough he had to be the one to check the receptionist was under. Even though Dutt the asshole said she knew it was to happen it didn't make Michael feel any easier about it. The saving grace was the department was close to finding out what was going on and he could shower away the nasty sensation of skullduggery.

"Are you sure that it's impossible to tell there's a body in the sand?" Michael said in a tone that made it sound as if wasn't really that important one way or another. "You know, bones and bits."

Dutt slowed the van as they rounded the last corner before their destination. "For fuck's sake. What the hell d'you think we go to the fucking quarry for? 'Cos we're fucking geogr…goe…oh fuck it, rock studiers or something?"

Michael shrugged. "Just asking." Something told him not to correct Dutt the A's language. Regarding geologists or the boring use of fuck every other word. "It's all a bit above me."

"Yeah well." Dutt sniggered, as he took Michael's words at face value and didn't see the irony in them. "Some of us know these things. Rings removed and all that. So, when it's all crushed it can go in with the coloring and no one will notice impuri…thingies. Sorted."

That was what Michael was worried about. Who was sorted and why? What was Dutt mixed up in and with whom? And he guessed, why? Not so coincidentally, he'd come across his old school mate 'accidentally' in Dutt's local, the night after Dutt's usual companion had suffered an unfortunate accident—with a group of the town's alleged unfinest and an iron bar. Dutt hadn't seen anything untoward about Michael's story of being down on his luck. After a couple of pints 'for old times' sake' Dutt offered him a driving job. Cash in hand, local deliveries and no questions asked on either side. It had been surprisingly easy. So much so, Michael had wondered if it was a trap. However, so far it seemed not. He'd driven the van around the town and most of Yorkshire over the previous two months and nothing had seemed out of place or even remotely dodgy. Mainly delivering wine, beer and small boxes of what Dutt said were seeds from a local garden center. One of the other operatives from Michael's section had managed a quick look one night and said that so far everything was as Michael had been told. Except a lot of the garden center boxes were full of sand and grit. One shift, if you could call it that, he'd been told to wait with the van whilst Dutt had accompanied some bloke with his beanie pulled way over his forehead to wherever. He'd only been gone around ten minutes and as far as Michael could tell hadn't been carrying anything. But he had returned in high spirits, given Michael a fifty with the proviso that it was just for hard work, not a bribe to turn a blind eye. That of course intrigued him and his bosses more than ever.

Then out of the blue, Dutt had asked him if he could 'pull an all-nighter'. Double pay, no details until he agreed. The way he looked at Michael set every alarm bell he knew ringing loudly.

"Yeah, I've nowt on," Michael responded laconically, aware of how his pulse had jumped and raced. "Just give me what I need to know. That'll do."

"What the fuck happened since good old grammar?" Dutt asked in a suspicious tone. "You know I always thought you were a fucking bloody goody two shoes at school."

"Good," Michael said before Dutt could voice any more suspicions. "That was what I hoped people thought. Guess it worked. Well, for a while. Fucking fuzz saw through it though."

Dutt guffawed. It sounded like a demented hyena. "Yeah?"

"Yeah, five years for…well never mind for what." His cover story would stand up to any scrutiny, his superiors had seen to that. "Got out of the clink, and got the fuck out of Britain. Until I had to come back. Too hot where I was." He hoped Dutt would take the words used with regards to illegal doings, not the weather. As Dutt smirked and winked it seemed he had.

"And here you are? Driving a smashed up body about." Dutt had told Michael oh so casually what he was to transport and obviously waited for his response. As Dutt had no doubt delved into Michael's alleged past, he reckoned there would be no arguments forthcoming. There hadn't been.

Michael nodded as the van drew up outside the gates of a local glassworks. "Apparently so. This the place?"

Dutt's phone rang and he swore as he fished it out of his pocket. "Hold on, this could be important. Yeah. Shite, okay." He turned to Michael and looked at him carefully. Michael distrusted the expression on his face.

"Yeah, this is it. You get out here. I'll take over. You go around the side and in through the tiny gate. It's been unlocked. Sodding Katrina's not on, so you need to check whoever it is, isn't awake or whatever. Bernie said all the coffee was doctored but he's not sure it worked. God knows why, it always has done in the past."

"Maybe she prefers tea," Michael said succinctly, as he wondered what else he was going to have to do to some unsuspecting woman.

"Maybe, but whatever, you need to sort her out. You know how?"

Michael shrugged. "Yeah. Then?"

"Come to the gateman's hut. We'll take it from there."

And if that wasn't designed to drop him in it, he didn't know what was. However, it seemed it was the breakthrough they'd been waiting for. Michael nodded as he got out of the van and headed where Dutt the A had indicated. As he pushed open the unlocked gate and slipped inside the grounds, he realized he had no idea how anyone could check for human remains in the cargo the van carried. He had to hope the powers that be had that covered. If not he could do damned all about it.

The shadows cast by the lone lamp were perfect for him to make his way, hopefully unseen, towards the brightly lit reception area. Inside he could see the back of the head of a blonde woman sat behind a desk, idly swinging her chair.

A tingle spiraled up his spine, and he stopped suddenly to scan his surroundings. Why that itch then? What made his body go on high alert?

Dutt and the van weren't through the gates yet. To all intents and purposes it was only him and the unknown woman about. Even the furnace building looked quiet, although he knew it wasn't.

But he'd learned by mistake never to ignore that itch. Michael changed direction until he was to one side of the glass doors and made for a small open window at shoulder height. He studied it and considered. It was unlikely to be a trap and he'd used smaller apertures to get into buildings in the past. It would do. Plus he never liked to stick to someone else's plan if he hadn't had a proper chance to go over it. This was very much flying by the seat of his pants stuff. Michael wasn't impressed with Dutt's brain or business acumen and to his way of thinking Dutt relied on chance and other people way too much. Whatever the man said, he couldn't imagine anyone meekly letting an unknown bloke dope her, be it the missing Katrina or someone else.

He angled his way through the window. Typically it was the window of a loo, and he was head first over a urinal. By the overwhelming smell of bleach the room had recently been cleaned. So he wouldn't be overcome by the smell of pee, just cleaning materials.

Michael thanked all the gods his agility was still reasonably good, and held his breath—he really didn't want to be found headfirst in a urinal—as he swung sideways across the porcelain and landed on his feet between a sink and a toilet stall. He tugged his t-shirt back into place and ran his hand through his hair. It needed cutting, the ends were beginning to curl. Next stop he guessed was Katrina's stand-in, and no fondling any of her, either. So not his thing.

As he walked quietly along the corridor he could hear a woman muttering. Her words made him grin.

"Why oh why do I let myself in for these things? Why can't I just say no? This is so not good and I can't even drink the coffee. God." She sounded disgusted—and familiar? Why did he know that voice? It couldn't be, surely…?

"What have I done to deserve this?"

"I have no idea, sweetie. What have you done?" Michael drawled as he walked into the foyer.

She gasped, shrieked and spun around to face him.

It was his turn to gasp. "Lindsey? What the hell…?"

"I should be asking you that," she said as she clutched her throat. "God almighty, what are you doing to me?"

He raised one eyebrow and took the three steps to stand inches in front of her, pulled her chair back so it wasn't in direct view of anyone who cared to look, and spun it around three times. She grabbed the arms and moaned. "Don't, for pity's sake. I feel sick enough as it is. Bloody coffee."

"Well, you'll feel a lot worse later, I guess." He steadied the chair by means of putting his foot on the base, and stared at her. "So why have you changed your name?" No one had mentioned her to him, and he'd been given a list of all employees by his boss. Or had he? He wouldn't put it past the man to miss out people if he thought it was in his department's best interest to keep some of the operatives in the dark over certain things.

Bastard.

"Eh? I haven't," Lindsey protested. "Apart from using my maiden name."

Something stunk. He hadn't seen Earnshaw on the list either.

"So why no Katrina? Did she ask you to cover for her?" If she had, it just added one more level of shittery to the night.

"Kat... Oh she's off sick. Fell off her horse and broke her ankle," Lindsey said. "I was asked to cover by Gary the bossman."

"Ah." *Oh shit.* Gary, who they thought had nothing to do with whatever was going on. Was this where Michael found himself duped?

"Ah what?" she said in a suspicious voice. "As in 'ah what are you doing here?'"

He had to give her marks for keeping her head. Her voice was steady, and unless you knew her shows and tells as he did, you would have no idea that she was tense, worried and puzzled.

"Nope, as in ah, I guess you don't know what someone, not me," he hastened to add, "has lined up for you tonight?"

She blinked and yawned. "Apart from terminal boredom as ever? Not a scooby. Hell, why do I feel like I'm in a dream or a nightmare? I can hardly keep my eyes open. And someone seems to have replaced my coffee with crap. It tastes disgusting and the gateman's isn't much better. So unless it's poisoning me with coffee, no idea who what or what."

"Doping, not poisoning. But you were supposed to be Katrina and obliging enough to be up for it." He ignored her muttered gasp and 'sod the lot of them' curse. "As you're not—Katrina or up for it—I guess the coffee was a sort of softening up, and I'm the sap they decided could take the fall if it all goes pear shaped." He didn't mention the fact that wasn't a likely scenario. Even murder was acceptable as a Dispatcher. As long as you did it tidily.

"What?" She bit her lip and then sniggered. "Michael, have you been on the pop? Why on earth…" Her eyes widened. "Oh fuck. You're one of them. I'm about to be screwed." She stood up and stepped behind her chair. "Stay away from me."

"Actually that's the one thing you're not. Screwed," he added at her blank expression. "I've been told I could touch the lovely Katrina up but no screwing. Her substitute wasn't mentioned in those terms." Michael went over everything he knew rapidly. He had two choices. Tell her the truth and hope she believed him and worked with him, or leave the status quo as it was and to hell with her or him, and hope whatever went down helped the department. He remembered her words.

"One of whom?" he asked as he reached over the chair, grabbed a handful of hair and tugged hard. Her eyes dilated and his cock hardened. It was still there. That part of them he missed as much as he missed her.

"Pet." He used the sobriquet on purpose and was more than happy to see her look down. It had to be a good sign. She still wanted him, wanted what they had once enjoyed. That Dom/sub relationship that never faltered until the very end. "Maybe we both better come clean."

"Maybe about what?" Lindsey said warily.

"Who we both are, why we're here, and the fact that within the next," he looked at his watch, "five minutes, I'm supposed to drug you so you can allegedly say you knew nothing about what's going on."

"But I don't," Lindsey protested. "I'm in the dark."

"I realize that, but evidently Katrina wasn't. And as no one knows we know each other, I'm expected to put you out so we can carry on."

"And then what?" Lindsey asked suspiciously. "What next?"

"I go help deliver the sand and frit."

"But that's tomorrow," she said puzzled. "It's in the diary."

"No one told the delivery men then," Michael said. "I was asked to pull an all-nighter. First one."

"Men?" She sounded as puzzled as he was.

What the hell was going on? Well, apart from dead bodies in the sand. Michael shrugged. "Yeah. I'm just a driver. Dutt the Asshole is the whatever you want to call him."

Lindsey's eyes opened wide, and she leaned on the back of the chair. "Dutt the Fuck? My not mourned, long departed ex? The guy who is supposed to start here as a night foreman tomorrow? Well sod it."

"Your... God almighty, why didn't I know that?" He could kick himself. It was an unusual name, so someone knew.

"It wasn't one of my finest moments," she said wryly. "Luckily I realized the error of my judgment before we tied the knot. But he's still an ex. Another facet of my ill-chosen men."

Intimating he was another one? A bit harsh, maybe? Okay, he had been given no reason to suspect Lindsey was here, and deliberately hadn't kept track of her once they split, but…

As he suspected, Darke *must* have known. Why hadn't the sod said anything? *Because he'd prefer to leave us both in the dark. Darke!*

"Damn it, I've been driving small deliveries all over Yorkshire for him these past weeks and I never knew. Someone should have told me."

"No whisky company then?" she said sarcastically. "Fancy that."

He shrugged again. He guessed she was entitled to have her digs at him. "Look, Lins, as you so rightly told me before you left, I wasn't entirely truthful. If I go full on honest now it might or might not be good for you. But as, with or without your help, I'm gonna put you under in a few moments, I'll open up, as long as you do. What is going on?"

"I don't know." She shook her head in disgust. "Boy, I wish I did. I've only been here a few weeks. I, er, was between jobs and Da…dammit, needed some money."

Hmm. All of a sudden things began to fall into place. *Da…? Darke?* "Darke by name and dark by nature," he said ambiguously. If she worked for them she'd know what he meant. Otherwise he'd have to go ahead with Dutt's plans and try to discover everything later.

Her eyes were as round as saucers. "Dark as night and dark as they come."

"Bloody hell," they both said together.

Lindsey flexed her fingers. "Sod the bastard. Do you want to kill him as much as I do?"

"Frequently," Michael said drily. "But for now, as we're on the same side, I'll put you under. Shallow so you won't be totally out of it. Just act as if you are. We'll have to play it by ear. What were you told to look out for?"

"Anything untoward. Bodies in the sand and stuff. You know, normal things like that." She grinned. "Nothing exciting."

"Oh we've one of them," he said grim and mirthless, as her eyes widened. "But it's been pounded to bits in a quarry first. I've been told it is impossible to find it. No idea what else is going on. Or why he put us both on the job." Darke knew he'd been married and to whom. Was this part of some Machiavellian plot only Darke was privy to?

"So to see things from all angles maybe?" Lindsey suggested. "After all, all I got told was, they suspected the Glassworks was involved in some way. Not specifically who or why. Then tonight I got a 'be aware' message and found out Dutt the fuck was due to start work here tomorrow. All in all, not good news. Now you turn up."

She didn't say if that was part of the shit or not. Michael studied Lindsey for a long moment, loath to make the next move, knowing he had no option. "Right, time to get moving. If I can't get back tonight where shall I meet you?"

She rattled off an address. Michael laughed. He might have guessed.

"Fancy that. You're two doors down from me."
Darke must be sniggering in his coffee.

Chapter Four

The voices ebbed and flowed around her. Pleased she'd had the forethought to let her head slump onto her folded arms, Lindsey listened as best she could to what Michael and someone whose tones she recognized as belonging to Dutt were saying. The third voice was that of Bernie the gateman.

"So dump it over by number two. It'll be in and used on Friday," Dutt said in his usual harsh crackly tone. "I'll be here then and make sure of it. With frit for black bottles no one would ever have a clue what their whisky or whatever is held in." He sniggered. "Wonder if it adds to the flavor."

Asshole is aptly named.

"'Kay. Where's number two?" Michael asked. "Remember it's my first time. I'll know next." He sounded confident, as if there was no question about a further visit by him. Lindsey mentally applauded his acting. Not by any inflection had he indicated he knew Lindsey when he'd indicated it was safe for Dutt to come in.

"Oh for fuck's sake," Dutt snarled. "Groping Miss Whoever here must have addled your wits. Where it says two. Bernie'll show you."

"Far end," Bernie said laconically. "Empty hopper. Just leave it there. I'll square it if anyone says anything. Shouldn't though, 'acos the lads emptied it once Gary had gone and spread it around the others. He'll be none the wiser come the morning. Sand there when he left, sand there when he gets back. Simple."

"Like you, Coultery-boy. Still it's all sorted," Dutt said in satisfaction. "Chop-chop, Coultery. Let's get it done and dusted. The missus will be waiting back home, spread legged and horny as hell. I slipped her a little something to get her revved up." He winked and snorted. "Once she gets going she's a belter. Thighs like a clamp."

God, he is an asshole. If it were possible to grit her teeth without moving, Lindsey would have done it. What a lucky escape she'd had. At least in their short-lived relationship Dutt had never gone down that route. Thank god she balked at actually saying 'I do' and got out before things had progressed that far. Living with the asshole for a few days had been bad enough. Lindsey knew what he'd expected and conjured up a job at the other end of the country, and firmly told him it was over. Dutt had gone abroad straight after, which made her suspect she was just a bit on the side to fill in his time until he did what he'd always intended to do. But now he was back in her orbit and she wanted him out as soon as possible. At least she was forewarned. He, she reckoned, was not.

Michael grunted and there was the sound of the door opening.

"Best get back to the gate, Bernie old boy. I'll check on Miss Whoever."

Oh hell. It was bloody hard *not* to react. What she'd like to do was use a rusty penknife on his balls. Slowly.

One day.

"Lindsey," Bernie said. "Nice lass is the new girl. Brings in cakes and stuff. Good cook."

"Fucking hell!" Dutt sounded incredulous. "Brings in cakes and stuff," he mimicked. "And lets you cop a feel? Why the hell didn't you say? I told poor Coultery here Katrina was the one to feel up, not Miss Newbie."

"Not at all," Bernie said with a snap of temper Lindsey had never heard before. "This lass is sound."

"Fuck it. Let me see." Why, he didn't say.

Lindsey relaxed as her head was rudely pushed up and dropped none too gently back on her arms. Then Dutt began to laugh. "Well bloody hell and ha sodding ha. Whoever would have thought it? The fair and iron-knickered Lindsey. Well, well, well. I wonder how far Coultery would have got with a grope there? Not far I bet. Ah well, as long as she's out, she won't know what hit her."

Oh yes she did. His hand. How she kept from saying something or taking her own swipe she had no idea.

Luckily the blow was enough to make her ears ring, and the sound of the door banging showed one or both of them had left. So how long did she have to pretend she was out of it?

Actually, she decided, as a headache of magnificent horrendousness began to make her head throb and her mouth dry, she might just as well let it take over. Lindsey relaxed and let whatever it was fill her consciousness.

She had no idea how much time passed before someone shook her gently.

"G'way. Sleepy."

"No you're not. You need to be awake now. Come on lass, you can't be seen sleeping on duty, now can you?"

Blearily she opened her eyes. Bernie stood in front of her. "Eh, lass, are you all right? When I saw you like this I thought I'd best pop in. Not like you to fall asleep? Bored were you?" His eyes were bright and inquisitive. "It's a long night, eh?"

"Ah yeah. I'm sorry." She did her best to sound embarrassed, and smothered a fake yawn. It wasn't sleep that made her feel like a half shut knife. "You won't tell on me, will you? I need this job. It's just it was an extra night and I wasn't ready for it."

"Bless you, you're all right." Bernie patted her arm. "Happens to the best of us. Now you go and wash your face, eh? Next shift will be on in an hour. You best make sure there's nothing for you to do."

She nodded, picked up her bag and made her way to the ladies. Someone had done a number on her and she was damned sure it wasn't Michael. If he said only just under, he meant it. Well he better have, because if on the off chance he was the miscreant and she found out, his nuts were going to be a fond memory. Never mind balls like walnuts. His would be peanuts. Crushed ones at that.

Before then though, she needed to fathom out how the hell had that one blow from Dutt plus whatever caused her to be out of it for so long? She looked at her watch. Five hours. Not possible, surely? She went for a pee, washed her hands and face and took a risk with swirling water around her mouth. Somehow, she didn't think they would have gone to such extremes as to put something in the main water supply. With a critical glance at herself, still pale with eyes like saucers and pupils like pin pricks, Lindsey fished in her handbag for some blusher, lippy and a hairbrush. That would do. Her shift was over in less than an hour. Then she could go home, nurse her headache and think everything over. Hopefully there wouldn't be any police spot checks or they'd definitely be doing a drugs test on her, and after Michael's warning, she wasn't sure they hadn't managed to get some sort of dope in her. Even so she would have to risk driving the few miles home. It was that or shanks pony, and in her state, shanks and his pony would be useless. Her legs were wobbly.

Surprisingly, everything after that point went smoothly and by 8 am she was unlocking her door and planning breakfast and bed. All she needed to do was turn off the alarm and…

It hadn't sounded. For the first time ever she'd been so preoccupied with her rehash of the night's activities she hadn't gone through her usual precautionary checks before she opened the door and now…

No alarm. Her nerves jangled as she gathered her scattered wits. *Think. What next?*

"Took you long enough."

Lindsey gasped, dropped her handbag on the floor and threw her shoulder bag—heavy with an assortment of bits and bobs she thought she might need to keep her awake during her shift—toward the voice. At the same time she whirled around and fumbled to hold her keys steady, with the sharp ends protruding between her fingers.

"How the hell did you get in here?" she asked in a harsh voice she didn't recognize as hers. "It was locked."

Michael heaved himself off the wall where he'd been waiting and took one step toward her. As ever his honed body made her pulse jitter and her mouth grow dry.

"Through the door. Your security is crap, pet. It took me less than a minute to get in and check the alarm, which incidentally you hadn't set. Whoever told you that was enough should be strung up by the balls."

"You tell him then. I'm sure the powers that be will be interested in your opinion."

"The Boss?"

Lindsey nodded. "The very same."

Michael shook his head. "What planet was he on? A kid with a toy set of lock picks could have got through the door without much trouble. Crazy."

"Planet 'I'm not to supposed to be anything other than an ordinary working girl who likes normal security precautions'—not those good enough to foil Darke's men. And usually I'd know if anyone was around."

Michael inclined his head. "Point taken. But surely an ordinary working girl remembers to set her alarm?"

"Good." Lindsey picked up her handbag and nodded towards the kitchen door, intent on a cuppa and a stern talking to him, for intruding, and herself for not realizing he—or anyone—was around where they shouldn't have been. "Hold on." She replayed his words. "I did set my alarm. I assumed you'd unset it."

Michael grabbed her arm before she reached for the door handle. "Are you sure, Lins? Really sure?"

Lindsey began to nod indignantly then forced herself to relax and replay her exit the evening before. "As sure as I can be," she said slowly. "I have a routine I go through. Nothing disturbed me as I did it. And, I only come out, lock the door and put my keys away once I've seen the flashing light go to the steady blink it does when it's set." She cast her mind back to leaving the house and walking to her car. "It was set."

"Then hold on, because it as sure as hell wasn't when I got in."

Her heart missed a beat. "Which means?" *Idiot. I know fine well what it means.* That thought was as damned scary as the idea Michael was standing in front of her once more. Of course, her body had reacted predictably, until her nipples hurt and her pussy muscles clenched and unclenched as if to remind her what they would like to do, given half the chance. It was all *she* could do not to fall into sub mode.

Long past and don't forget it.

She risked a quick glance at him, and wished she hadn't. In the shadowy hallway his blond hair, short—although some tiny curls were showing—with just a hint of red at the tips stood out, and contrasted with the inevitable dark t-shirt and worn denims that were molded to his thighs and white along the seams. The man of her dreams. The man she has once willingly, lovingly, called her Sir.

And, she allowed as some of the less pleasant memories bombarded her, also her nightmares.

He nodded toward her alarm, silent and watchful. "Someone's been here," he said quietly. "Not here now, though. I checked when I realized it wasn't on. Now who and why?"

"I wish I knew. Lord, if only my head wasn't still so fuzzy, I might be able to think properly." She pressed her hands to her eyes and blinked rapidly. That not-quite-with-it sensation was still there. "What now?"

"We check if you can see anything out of place. And maybe you make a coffee?"

She shuddered. "Tea. After the sludge they tried to call coffee last night I'm…fuck. That bloody coffee." Lindsey clenched her fists and then had to force herself not to slam one or both down onto something hard. "No wonder Bernie kept looking at me strangely when I was still upright and reasonably sensible. I bet I was supposed to be out for the count by that alone. You were the precaution."

"A way of tying me into the shit," Michael said positively. "After we'd unloaded, Dutt the Fuck was about crowing. I reckon they'd turned the security cameras on so I was shown as doing the dirties. Pity for them, I nipped back and disabled everything once I'd been dropped off. So, we never got around to discussing the coffee."

Lindsey shuddered theatrically. "It was so goddamn awful I poured it down the sink."

Michael opened the door to the kitchen. "I

promise my coffee won't be tampered with." He turned back to her, still standing in the hallway, and propelled her into the room she used most when she was at home. "Sit down before you fall down. You look like death warmed up."

"Jeez, thanks. How to make a girl feel good." But she did as he bade her, glad not to have to show her weakness. A swift glance in the mirror told her he wasn't exaggerating. She did look as bad as she felt.

Michael filled the kettle and switched it on. "Paracetamol? Or any painkillers?"

"Third drawer down. Why, do you have a headache?"

He fished the packet out and handed two tablets to her with a glass of water. "Nope. You do, though. Take these, pet, I need you to be alert. Look around and see if anything looks different or out of place." He picked up her blue and red spotted teapot, rummaged in the cupboard and found the tea. "You still use loose leaves then."

Lindsey nodded. "Duh, I hate tea bags."

"I remember the hissy fit when that was all we had."

She blushed. "Yeah, a bit over the top, I admit, but call me old-fashioned, I so prefer leaves."

Michael warmed the pot and spooned tea leaves into it. "Take your tablets. Miss Old-Fashioned and take your time looking around. It's important."

She, sniggered, swallowed the tablets obediently and slowly perused her kitchen. Everything seemed in place. The clock on the second shelf of the dresser was still slightly skewed, just as Darke had suggested. The third drawer down was partially open with a dishcloth seemingly thrown over the handle. Even her frog timer was as it should be.

"Everything appears to be fine." Her eyes narrowed and her gaze homed in on the paper she'd left on the table. "Except the newspaper. And pencil. It wasn't like that." She'd ruffled the sheets a bit, and left the pencil at a specific angle. More alert now, Lindsey began another slow look around the room. "I can't see anything else," she said at last. "Just the paper."

Michael nodded as he poured boiling water into the teapot. "While this brews are you up to checking everywhere else?"

In reply she stood up and tucked an errant curl behind her ear. "Yeah. And if anyone has had their grubby paws on my underwear I'm indenting the department. For La Perla, at least."

Michael shoved the tea cozy over the pot and laughed. "Don't blame you. I'll sign the chit. Right, come on. You look ready for bed."

I would be if you were in it with me. Thank god she hadn't said that out loud. Lindsey nodded. "It's been an eventful night. When I signed up I was told it would be humdrum and repetitive. If being drugged and knocked out is the repetition bit, they can shove their job where the sun doesn't shine."

"Fair enough."

Chapter Five

"I honestly can't see anything where it shouldn't be," she said as they reentered the kitchen. "But I don't know, something doesn't feel right. As my gran used to say, it's a feeling in my water." She laughed, self-conscious at her attitude. "Stupid, eh? But the newspaper was definitely not like that, and I *did* set the alarm. So who what and why?"

Michael leaned against the sink, crossed his legs at the ankles and sipped his tea while he studied her thoughtfully. He'd checked as best he could, seen no bugs or anything obviously planted, but he didn't know just what she had in her home. He had an idea or two, why someone had searched, but how much to divulge and how much to keep to himself? He rather thought it had just been a precaution after Dutt and whoever found out she was on duty, and wanted to be sure it was by accident not design. Now he was in a dilemma. In some ways it went against the grain not to explain to her, a fellow operative, what he had deduced, but on the other hand, she wasn't a Dispatcher per se, even if Darke was the boss of them both. Only a very elite few belonged to that covert, never to be mentioned group.

"Do you know what a Dispatcher is?" he asked conversationally. "In any form."

Lindsey's greeny-blue eyes darkened. "Someone who dispatches things," she said and chuckled. "Unspecified things." She set her cup down on the table. "Why?"

"Wondered." How much did she know? "Have you heard of that department?" He continued to stare at her, eyes narrowed. It didn't seem to unnerve her, nor had he expected it to. Anyone who worked for Darke would take such a scrutiny in their stride.

"Hmm, is this one of those damned if I have, damned if I haven't moments?" she asked. "You know, of the 'I'll show you mine if you show me yours' variety. "Because if it is, you go first. Age before beauty." *Dom before sub.*

"Lindsey." He spoke flatly with a hint of command in his tone. "This is no joke. I need to know exactly what you do know and what's been expected of you. Now, pet, remember who I am. Tell me what I want to know."

It wasn't the words but the tone that brought her up short. Michael the Dom was back in spades.

"I know very little," she said honestly. "I was recruited and after a few jobs of keeping my eye, and writing reports on odds and sods, like a betting shop with illegal goings on, and some twerp who thought he could try and blackmail an MP, I was asked to apply for the night receptionist at the Glassworks. My specialty is numbers. I've no idea how Darke arranged for me to get this job, or if I was the only one who applied, but up until tonight it was uneventful. I've never been so bored in my life. Watching paint dry would be more interesting."

"I can so see that." Michael was sure Darke would have somehow arranged it as he intended. He usually did. "Anything else?"

She shook her head and those damned curls bounced around like they had a life of their own. Were they as long as they used to be? He hoped so.

Why? It was over. Even so, his cock was ready to argue with his common sense. It ached as he remembered just what he had so often used the long tresses for. Would he ever get the opportunity again? Lord, he hoped so. He had to be suffering blue balls for a reason.

"Should there be more? Is this anything to do with

why you were never around when we were," she waved one hand in the air, "you know."

"Married," he said wryly. "Yes and no. I was in a different department, but in essence yes, I worked covertly for the government. Nowadays I'm based nearer to home. Where were you for your training?"

She stared at him, put her cup down and began to tap her fingers impatiently on the tabletop. "Surely, Mr. Spy Man, you should know."

Sassy.

"Not necessarily. And…fuck." His pocket vibrated. "This conversation isn't over." He tugged his phone up to the top of his pocket. As ever it jammed on the double denim rim and he swore ripely. What he saw on the screen made him swear again.

'Dark Isle, needed.' Michael switched the screen off and put the phone away. *He* would need both hands free to do what was necessary.

"Right, the conversation will have to be continued later." Michael pulled Lindsey to her feet. "Come on, we need to be somewhere else like ten minutes ago. You've been rumbled." He grabbed her arm and frog-marched her to the back door, happy her house was a carbon copy of his.

"Rumbled what? Hey where's the fire and what the hell?" Lindsey began to resist. "I'm not going anywhere without an explanation." She used her free arm to hold onto the sink. Michael glared. It had no effect on his companion, except her eyes flashed a message of retribution. He began to worry if he'd ever have the opportunity to father children.

"Can't we see what's going to happen?"

"We have no time." He didn't add 'not unless you want to leave in a body bag'. That might be a bit melodramatic. Maybe.

"Make time," she said implacably. "Or I'll scream blue murder."

They didn't *have* time for that. With a mental apology to her—again—Michael applied pressure to Lindsey's neck and as she sagged, caught her and put her over his shoulder. Sadly not the occasion to paddle her perfect ass until she was deep in sub space. Or even spitting tacks and sweating to have his balls in a vise. He didn't even have time to grab her any of her non-violated underwear. They had to move. Darke's message was unequivocal. 'Move and fast. Enemy not to be approached. Usual route.' Why, he didn't know, nor at that moment in time did he much care. Darke was the boss and would have his reasons.

Michael reckoned they had half an hour tops. To get into his hidden car, get the hell out of Dodge and be ready for her temper when she woke up.

God, why hadn't he stuck to theology?

****

Shit and hellfire. Why did she feel like crap again? Why was the earth moving? And why did she hate the word why? If it were possible Lindsey would have sniggered. Why was the one word that rarely got a straightforward reply? It was longer than she cared to remember since the earth had moved for her, and it was unlikely that was this her lucky day. Was she at last getting some…? Her brain began to function. Why was her bed on a slant and her pillow both soft and rock hard? Almost like a shoulder.

A shoulder. Not a pillow, a shoulder. It is a bloody shoulder. What the hell? With difficulty Lindsey opened her eyes. Darkness. Pitch black darkness. Like a velvet shroud.

Nope. Do not think of shrouds.

However, darkness? She couldn't have slept until

it was nighttime surely? And she had to be at work and be on the lookout for dead bodies… Dead bodies.

Voices filtered into her consciousness. Something about pigs and who was on duty. Someone laughed, and it wasn't a pleasant sound.

"Yeah sure is pigs, and Mac I think."

Another speaker this time; one whose voice she didn't recognize. A hint of a Scottish accent maybe? The only person she'd met in the organization with that accent was Darke and it was definitely not him.

"He was just saying they were in need of fresh meat."

"This meat is rotten to the core," Michael said with a hint of laughter in the timbre of his voice. "Poor pigs."

"Ach, they'll eat anything fresh or rotten, you know them. Not picky."

Pigs? Fresh meat? God; am I in a horror film and no one's told me? Lindsey moaned and tried to see. Something was covering her eyes surely? It couldn't be pitch black. Not in England. Streetlights, car lights, shops, and pubs. Traffic lights and light pollution. Even in the country there was always a glow from somewhere.

"Hold on." The voice *was* familiar and definitely who she thought it was.

"Michael." She made sure it wasn't a question. The events of what she assumed was the previous night came rushing back to her. "What's going on?" She did her best to move her arms, and found that they wouldn't cooperate. "What have you done to me? Sir, we don't play like this, I'm red…" Her voice trailed off as someone else snorted with laughter.

"Fuck you," Lindsey said clearly and defiantly as she realized what she'd said. "We don't play at all," she said flatly. "We aren't a 'we' any more." In truth she wondered if, apart from BDSM, they ever had been. There they had meshed in every way possible. Outside their play…she mentally shrugged. What time they had spent together had at first been good. Then, as it got less and less and Michael got ever more secretive, suspicion crept in.

It hadn't taken long for their play to stop and for her to issue her ultimatum.

Do not go there. It's over. Concentrate on now and why.

Somewhere a less arsy chuckle was cut off abruptly. Then she heard a third voice murmur. "That's your Dom cred down the toilet then, mate."

Who else was with them? Or should that be how many who elses?

"Lins, if you give me five minutes I'll untie you," Michael said briskly in a no-nonsense way. "Just be patient."

"My middle name," she said acerbically and hoped her confusion didn't show. No pet for now then. Should that make her happy or sad? Lindsey couldn't fathom that one out.

"Right, and mine is sub," Michael said dryly. "Not. So hold on until we get round this corner," he added. "And, yeah here we are." The car—she assumed it was a car—slowed, and her shoulder pillow moved so her cheek rested on a leather headrest.

"Oh good," Lindsey said sarcastically. "Now if only I knew where here was I could rest happy." There was that arsy snort gain. "Pigs in the car are there?" she said sweetly. "Oink, snort and all that."

"Enough." That was Michael's Dom's voice. "Politeness is preferable."

"Politeness has to be earned," she said snippily and ignored the pull of need and submission that swept through her. "No earning as far as I can hear."

She could almost feel his glare, and she shivered. Why was she goading him for a reaction? Would she never learn? *Probably not.* Her mouth seemed to engage before her brain when he was around these days.

"Here is a private airstrip," Michael said, with a biting precision that under any other circumstances would have her on the floor, head bowed and contrite. "You don't need to know where it is."

"Nor who our not so charming companions are?" She'd already shown her antagonism and indifference—albeit feigned—so she didn't attempt to disguise the sarcasm.

"Nor that. They're leaving us now."

"Sadly," one voice said. "But now you're here we can do the mop up. Don't forget the baggage."

"Not likely. Over to you. Code Red. Carlos as pilot? Reception sorted?"

Did they always talk in shorthand or was it to foil her understanding of what was going on? If so they needn't have bothered; she hadn't got a clue.

"Who else. Milo will do the meet and greet, and grab the cargo. Everyone is already on red alert." There was a grunt, and a short bark of laughter. "Not that sort."

Now Lindsey did have a headache. As the car stopped, her seat dipped, fingers fumbled at her wrists and thankfully her hands were freed. She flexed them experimentally. Not too sore, so she had to assume she'd not been restrained for overlong. Long enough though. Pins and needles hit her and she gasped. It was so not on. They were only welcome as the result of play, not whatever this was.

Bastards. Lindsey rubbed her fingers, and made several fists to get rid of the nasty tingles. She hoped no one thought it was because she wanted to hit them, even though that was sounding a better option by the minute. This was the time to be subservient and acquiescent. Until she knew what was going on at least.

"Not long now, pet," Michael said reassuringly. "Then I'll take the blindfold off. Better for you all round if you remain in ignorance of this bit."

Her axis shifted as once more she was moved, this time to be helped out of the car and to stand swaying. One of her legs had gone to sleep and she did her best to get the circulation flowing once more. A warm and comforting hand held her steady, as her bum hit something hard, and then again the world spun as she was cradled in an unknown person's arm and the said person began to move.

This too-ing and fro-ing was a pain in the ass. Literally.

"Almost there, pet." Michael's voice so presumably his arms.

"Will you stop calling me that," she said fiercely, suddenly annoyed at him for bringing back too many memories. Lord, Lindsey thought, ashamed of herself, she was a contrary bitch. He was damned if he did and damned if he didn't. She needed to pull up her big girl knickers and get over it. Even so she just had to snipe back. "I'm not your pet. My name is Lindsey and you know it."

"You were my pet though."

How the hell could he sound so bloody reasonable? She wanted him to lose his temper, so she could retaliate.

"Were being the operative word."

"My sweet loving wife and sub. I like to call you pet."

"Ex wife. Masochistic tendencies?" she asked sweetly and he laughed.

"Trust you to push and prod even when the odds are stacked against you. What do you think?"

Well, no…he'd never been into masochism or sadism. Just sweet pain for pleasure. She shrugged. "Not up to me to say."

"Oh dear." His tone was mocking. "Nose out of joint, pet. If I had time I would remind you what happens to bratty subs. As I don't, hold the thought."

Lindsey let her breath out in a long hiss and Michael laughed. "Wet and wanting, love?"

That, she knew, was the problem. She was and her pussy muscles were doing the samba.

"Keep still. We're climbing the steps and the doorway is low," he warned her suddenly. "I don't want to give you unnecessary pain." Just pain we both like, his tone inferred. "Once you're settled we can head off." He didn't say where to and she was damned if she'd give him the satisfaction of knowing she was curious.

It was getting harder and harder to remember who they both now were. As her wits returned Lindsey began to accept what she'd suspected on and off all evening. She was as susceptible to him now as she'd ever been. *Damn.*

Lindsey felt herself gently deposited in a seat and then her blindfold was removed and she blinked in the soft illumination within a tiny plane cabin. Engines were humming gently in the background, and outside the window she could see lights flickering.

The outline of a man through the open door of the cockpit showed briefly as the glow outside shimmered and oscillated though the windscreen—if, she thought hazily, that was what you called it.

The plane swayed and the engine noise increased as Michael settled down in the seat beside her.

"You okay? Not too bad a head?" He sounded

concerned. Was it all put on or did he genuinely care?

She had no idea and it irked her. Lindsey hated being out of her depth.

"Hmm, no thanks to you." Hell, she sounded grumpy. "Why didn't you just tell me what to do?"

"You'd have argued."

He had a point, she conceded grudgingly, but the last thing she intended was to let him know she agreed with him. "Well it was all a bit melodramatic wasn't it?" She pitched her tone to sound amused and disinterested, and wasn't sure if she succeeded or not. Michael was a master at not showing his reactions. "I mean out of the back door and so on," she persisted. "How did we get here anyway? There was no back gate."

"Over the fence, through the allotments, and into a car I had there."

"Grief. Why?" Now she knew her astonishment showed. This new level of spy thing was more than a bit beyond her understanding. It was all too movies and TV dark dramas to be comfortable.

"We had no time. Three intruders were picked up not twenty minutes after we left. With weapons."

"And?" The plane began to taxi and Lindsey automatically tightened her seat belt over her churning stomach. Tin can flying wasn't her usual mode of transport. Give her an airbus any time with a gin and tonic and a packet of peanuts.

Michael grinned, and her heartbeat gave a funny little jump. That smile could light up a room, let alone a four-seater plane cabin. She loved the way his lips quirked more on one side than the other, and his green eyes narrowed and crinkled.

Down girl. Wait and see what's going on before you go all gooey.

"Don't know yet. The people who picked the

intruders up had no time to question anyone. That'll happen soon."

"So how will you find out what's going on?" Lindsey asked, interested in spite of herself. "If you're not there."

"Oh I'll be there," Michael assured her. "I wouldn't miss it for anything. This is my job. As for them? That's the cargo."

Chapter Six

After a journey that even the most hardened flyer couldn't call comfortable—wind, rain, and even the odd thundercloud far too close for comfort—Michael was more than impressed with how Lindsey had coped with the flight. He knew her flying limits, and a plane this size was as near red as dammit. However, he'd reasoned that a, they weren't in a scene, and b, needs must. The c, would have been to knock her out again, but he concluded that if he did that, his hopes of ever getting inside her again, or gaining her sweet submission, were less than zero.

However she was as white as the snow-capped hills they had flown over, and after the first few minutes of the flight had remained silent.

As Carlos shouted about side winds and hold on, Michael gripped Lindsey's hand. She returned the pressure so tightly he'd have crescent shaped scars where her nails dug in.

"You're doing fine, pet," he said reassuringly. "Almost there."

"Where?" It was the first words she'd spoken in over an hour. "Where's there?"

Her voice wasn't much above a strangled whisper, but he heard the anxiety in it.

"Scotland," he said. "Land of lochs, glens, mountains and midges. We're going to Dark Isle."

She harrumphed. "Dark Isle?"

"Also known by some as Death Isle. Take your pick."

"Clear as mud," Lindsey muttered. "Neither sounds welcoming."

So she hadn't done any training there. That, Michael thought, was interesting. Darke evidently had, as promised ages ago, started up a section apart from the Dispatchers, and kept the newbies in the dark about the Dark, so to speak.

"It's a safe place to interrogate the cargo," he said mildly. "And dispatch as necessary." He didn't add that their favored way of disposing traitors was to feed them—preferably live—to Mac's beloved pigs. He didn't think she'd swallow that easily.

"Only the cargo?"

He glanced at her quizzically. "Who else? Do you need interrogating?"

Lindsey shook her head and winced. "Nope, not at all. So, something is amiss, we're going to somewhere in Scotland, so someone can interrogate somebody?"

"That's about it."

"So why am I here?"

He wondered when she would get around to asking that. "Protection. It seems somehow, sometime recently you were sussed. Or suspicion cast on you for a reason. Is that enough somes?"

She sighed. "Yeah, more than enough. I thought I'd got a nice quiet job collecting information."

"As do lots of people, I guess. Blame the boss. He's a master manipulator. For, he will tell you, only the best of reasons. Mind you, it's true he has a knack of placing people where they will fit best."

"Hmm." She didn't sound convinced. "I can't see how being drugged is best for anyone. That scenario wasn't in my remit."

He wondered what had been.

"And," she said with an upward tilt of her eyebrows, "how about you?"

"I don't want to be drugged either."

"That," Lindsey said indignantly with a hint of her old sass and spark, "is not what I meant and you know it. What does he think suits you best?"

"Ask him. I'd bet my last oatcake he'll be waiting for us."

"I don't want to ask him, I'm asking you," Lindsey said snappily. "And I don't like oatcakes."

Michael bit back his intended warning about her attitude. He had to remember he no longer had the right to be her Sir. "It's not up to me. To paraphrase my mum, tough bananas, want must be your master."

"Not you?" She looked horrified. He was damn certain that *was* a Freudian slip.

He smiled. "Not at the moment, eh? Who knows what might happen once we've got all this cleared up." The plane landed with a gentle bump and taxied to a halt. "Okay, I'll be honest here. I either have to blindfold you or put you out again. Up to you."

"Why? Why can't I know where I'm going? I hate not being able to see." Her voice rose and he heard the beginning of panic set in. "It freaks me out."

"And breathe." Michael reached over, undid her seatbelt and stroked her cheek. "I'll be there for you I promise. It's not my idea, pet. I'm just the transporter. But…" He hesitated. What the hell, he'd already said more than he should. "In the interest of both your safety and others, it's better you don't know exactly how we get to where we're going."

"Dark Isle, somewhere in Scotland?"

"Maybe. Now do I blindfold you or…?"

"Not the or," she said hastily. "I have a woozy enough head as it is. I don't suppose I can convince you I'd keep my eyes shut?"

"Nope." Curiosity would be bound to get the better of her.

"Oh well, blindfold it is. When?"

Michael took the long strip of blackout material

from his jacket pocket. "Now."

****

They were on a boat. And it rocked. A lot. Why had she never suspected she would be seasick? Or if they were in Scotland as Michael intimated, should that be loch sick? Lindsey bit back a moan, swallowed heavily and cleared her dry throat. "In the words of any kid under twelve, are we there yet?" The boat lurched violently and she rolled onto her side. "Shit, I'm gonna throw up."

"No you're not, pet. Breathe deeply. Come on, go with it." Someone tapped her ass. "Or do you want me to take your mind off it?"

Michael.

It had to be said. "I need a pee as well."

Someone near muttered something she couldn't interpret.

"Five minutes and we'll be there. Oh, and we'll be out of the worst of the wind. Evidently a wee bit of a storm blew up unexpectedly." Michael—it had to be him, she recognized his particular male scent—kissed her clammy cheek and stroked her hair back off her face. "I'm sorry. I had no idea you got seasick."

"Loch sick," she said automatically, and heard him chuckle. "Nor did I. Know I mean. But then I guess I've never had the combination of being drugged, knocked out, a plane ride in a sardine can and a boat journey on a vessel the size of a bedside table before."

"Wardrobe, lass, at least a wardrobe."

The different voice meant there was a driver or whatever you called them, as well as Michael. "Wardrobe then. Who am I to differentiate? Whatever, it's bloody tiny. I prefer a cross channel ferry at the very least. And a jumbo or airbus."

"Peanuts and fizz?"

"Well duh…ugh…" The boat had turned sharply

and she would have hit the deck if Michael hadn't held her fast. His hand grazed her breast and she automatically leaned into his touch. For a brief second his fingers caressed the soft roundness and pinched her nipple so her pussy muscles clenched in anticipation of what next.

Predictable and fantastic.

Then the rocking motion slowed.

Damn! She could have done with a few more minutes. That touch had been possessive and her body yearned for more. Her nipples had turned into hard nubs, her clit throbbed and her panties were damp. She moaned softly and turned her head to find him.

"We're about to dock." His voice was soft and soothing. "Hold that thought," Michael murmured. "For later. For now we go and report."

Lindsey wondered just what she had to report, other than, 'Darke you bastard, you played me for a sucker'. Somehow she didn't think that would be an appropriate response. Even so, she nodded as Michael lifted her easily, and they moved from the boat to the shore. Within seconds her feet touched solid ground.

"Blindfold?" she asked.

"Soon." He swung her into his arms again. "Five minutes and we'll be there." The wind teased her hair and she spat several strands out before she was able to twist it and tuck it between them.

"Where's there?" She didn't hold out much hope for a definite answer, which was just as well. She didn't get one.

"Where we are going." He carried her easily, without many bumps or jolts. Once he swore and she was lowered slightly. "Tree branch," he said briefly, as leaves stroked her hands where they were clamped around his neck. "Sodding weather."

"At least it's not snowing," she said, and he

grunted.

"Yet."

They moved sideways and Michael's foot slipped. He recovered immediately. "Sorry. It's bloody muddy. Evidently it's rained every day, solidly, for a week. This track is almost impossible." His hand under her thighs tightened as he straightened and the other closed hard across her chest. Being that close without touching him and he responding in a loving way was hell. She forced herself not to stroke the nape of his neck, where her hands could discern soft fine hair. Not the time or the place.

"We were lucky to be able to come in the way we did. The other is twice as long and twice as uneven." His breathing was even and unlabored. No one would know he was carrying an adult. Okay, she wasn't over heavy but neither was she a lightweight. "Almost there."

Right then, not much point asking anything else. Just enjoy...or suffer. Lindsey let herself relax into Michael's hold and swayed easily as he began to climb. Not steps, but a slope. Then the sound of his footsteps changed, and the crunch of gravel was clearly heard.

The chill of the night air changed to warmth, and even behind her blindfold, the hint of brightness told her they were indoors.

Not a moment too soon. Her need to pee was becoming imperative. She raised her hand to where she hoped Michael was, found a material clad arm and clutched it.

"Take this damned thing off and let me go to the loo, please," she hissed as she was carefully settled onto her feet. At least this time she didn't have pins and needles or a dead leg. Just that imperative necessity to relieve herself. "I'm over the loch sickness but needs must."

The blindfold was removed and she blinked as the bright lights of wherever they were began to hit her. "Door on the left," Michael said as he threw his jacket over a nearby chair. "Give me your coat first. I'll wait here for you. Don't want you to get lost." Or go where you shouldn't, his tone intimated.

There was nothing she could do but nod and head for the door he indicated. Sure enough it led into a tiny cloakroom, just big enough for a loo, wash basin and vanity. After she'd used the facilities—and peed like an elephant—Lindsey glared in the oval mirror at the tangled mess laughingly called a hairstyle. She'd never gone for anything complicated, but bird's nest wasn't exactly flattering. Or easy to get rid of using her fingers. She did her best, and shuddered. It still looked a mess, damp and lank around her whiter than white face. Lindsey rubbed her cheeks to get some color into them, before heaving a great sigh. Best to go back and face whatever came next.

Michael was still where she had left him, threading the blindfold through his fingers. He saw her glancing at it and smiled. "Better things to use it for than that journey eh?"

Lindsey raised one eyebrow and hoped her instant arousal at his words didn't show. "As you say," she said equably. "So, what's next?" Now she was inquisitive. Nosy and needing to know what next. "Thumbscrews, or…" Shit! She nearly said nipple clamps. Those damned erotic thoughts that blindfold had conjured up. "The dripping water torture?"

"Not for you. We tidy up, eat and then go for a debriefing." He stretched out his hand and she took it. Michael grinned and pressed a kiss to the back before turning it over between his fingers and holding tight. "You're lucky it's usually the other way around. Darke must have heard your tummy rumble."

Lindsey covered that part of her body with her hand. "Oops. But yeah, I want a shower, clean clothes and food—in that order." She had a thought and groaned. "Do I have any clothes?"

"Not of your own," Michael said honestly. "There wasn't time to pack, but there will be stuff for you. New, before you ask and what will be useful up here. Jeans and warm socks and stuff."

"And fit?" she said, suspicious of his openness.

He grinned.

Damn, that smile does things to my insides that no self-respecting smile ought to do.

"Well of course," Michael said with a knowing wink. "We all know to beware of a woman not feeling her best. I'll add, before you go all suspicious, that I think Darke's lady will have sorted them as soon as I gave her your size. Which, yes, I got by sneaking a peek in your wardrobe before you got home. Love the red thong."

She was damned sure her face was the color of that item of clothing.

"Yes well, good, no not...I mean oh sod it." She punched Michael on the arm as he broke into a fit of laughter. "Stop sniggering or..."

"Or?"

She laughed with him. It was that or stamp her feet and throw a strop. Neither of which were grown up or professional. After all it was only a thong, for goodness' sake. Not crotchless knickers or a peekaboo bra. Hopefully he hadn't found them.

"Well or I dunno but I hold onto a good sulk." She rolled her eyes. "And they do say revenge is a dish served cold and all that."

"True, and honestly I only checked your size on the necessities. You haven't changed have you?"

"Nope." She was proud of that. "Well, not in a clothes size, anyway."

Michael shook his head. "Still sassy. Right, come on, and let me show you our quarters." He began to walk across the hallway. "Are you coming?" Michael turned and looked at her quizzically.

Lindsey hadn't moved. "Ours?"

"Ah. Yeah. You see, this facility doesn't have a lot of spare room at the moment. We're building on but nowhere is ready." He shrugged but the imp of mischievousness was apparent in his oh-so-innocent expression. "So it's share with me or a cell. As Dutt the fuck and his cronies are in most of them, I thought you'd prefer to be with me rather than them."

"Yeah, you have a point." But it stilled smelled of fish. "And two beds?"

Michael shook his head. "Nope, sorry just one, but it is a super king. My quarters aren't big enough for two bedrooms. And why would I want two anyway?"

That rung true, but the rest? "Then if it's super king I can get a pillow down the middle."

He stared at her for what seemed like ages but was probably only a couple of seconds. "You can, but seriously, will you want one?"

"Whether I want one or not is immaterial. It's that or you're on the floor. Or the couch." Lindsey wasn't giving him an advantage to do anything. She needed serious thinking time before she let him close.

He rolled his eyes. "A pillow it is."

"I thought you'd say that." She narrowed her eyes to look at him closely and mistrusted his oh-so-innocent expression. However, if he thought she'd change her mind he was sadly mistaken. There would have to be a lot more talk and negotiation before she got anywhere near to thinking even maybe.

"Right, so find the pillow and lead the way."

Chapter Seven

The noise of the shower brought back memories he really ought to suppress. Of holding her by her hair as, on a rare occasion she went down on him, water spraying over them, he coaxed her to go further. Loving it and hoping for more. Encouraging his pet. Taking her in the ass with them pressed hard against the glass shower wall and seeing their reflection in the anti-misting mirror outside the stall.

Her legs wrapped around him, his cock pulsing hard inside her, and watching her eyes glaze and hearing her mewls as he pumped his cum deep into her pussy.

Of hearing her sweet sighs of submission.

And of showering alone and jerking off as he remembered it all.

Michael fisted one hand into the other, relished the pain and thought of icy water, terrorists, greedy pigs, angry bosses or anything to deflate his cock. If there had been a handy wall he might have thumped it. Only the thought that his apartment had been newly renovated and the paint was hardly dry stopped him.

The sound of the water shutting off kept him from taking himself in hand. Seeing him rub one out was not the way to make her happy and comfortable in his presence. She was already as skittish as a kitten, and not in a good, BDSM way either. He needed to go slowly, be caring and thoughtful to what she preferred, if he wanted her to be his again. Showing himself as needy and horny wasn't going to display that side of him—he recognized that.

The bathroom door opened and his heart missed a beat as Lindsey wandered into the bedroom, covered from just above her breast to mid thigh in a large towel.

As she walked it opened, showed a tantalizing hint of the top of her legs, but sadly not quite enough to display what was hidden above there. She held another towel in her hands and rubbed it over her hair in an absent manner as she moved further into the room.

"Nice view, want to drop the towel?" He drawled the words, careful not to sound too dominant. Hopefully that would come later. Once they had sorted everything out. "Don't mind me, I'd enjoy the show."

She gaped and lifted her head. Then with what could only be called a mischievous smile, swung the towel in her hands in a circle about her head, and threw it insouciantly onto the bed. The towel around her torso stayed firmly in place, even though she thrust one leg out and stood in what could only be called an erotic model pose. One leg thrust through the gap in the remaining towel, and she put her hand on her fist.

"There," she purred the word, and his cock threatened to split the zipper on his jeans. So bloody come hither and teasing. "How's that?"

Michael shook his head. "You, pet, will be the death of me, I swear. If we had time I'd show you just how it is. Sadly, we need to get ready to face the music. Also known as Darke. He's waiting for us. Give me five to have a shower. Clothes in the cupboard over there." He waved towards a large wall cupboard, called a press in the area. "We seemed to have missed the opportunity to eat. Go check the clothes. Just basic, but perfect for here."

"Nothing is perfect about being told you're lacking," Lindsey said gloomily. "That you're a failure." She sighed. "Ouch." She rubbed her ass where Michael had landed his hand, none too gently. "That hurt."

"Stop lying," Michael said reprovingly and hid his smile as color rushed into her cheeks and she bit her lips.

"It didn't even sting very much. I'll be happy to show you what really hurts later. Now stop your silliness, and get ready. You haven't done badly. In fact I'm betting Darke will have one of his rare moments of praise."

"Really?" She sounded skeptical. "What did I do to deserve that? Let a body be disposed of?"

Michael pinched her earlobe, in the way he knew she would recognize. Their code for out of order. "Now enough of that. That wasn't down to you, pet, and you know it. You kept your head for a start." He smiled as she glared, gulped and then shrugged.

"Well, maybe."

"No maybe, you did exactly as you should. Right, dress, woman and let me go shower. Evidently once we've been grilled we will get a grill. Steak and chips." He flicked his pinkie over her cheek. "I'm ready for food to feed the body." He didn't add 'and hope to feed the soul later'. She obviously knew that, judging by the way her eyes widened and then she looked downwards. Michael chuckled. "We'll sort it all out." He headed to the bathroom without waiting for her comeback. He was in no doubt that there would be one.

The sound of something heavy hitting the floor made him chuckle. She'd found the walking boots then. If she didn't want them, Darke had recently installed under floor heating on the advice of the ladies who were attached to the various Dispatchers. They were adamant if they were supposed to go barefoot, they needed something to encourage them. Pleasing their Doms in this instance wasn't enough. He could empathize. Winter in Scotland wouldn't persuade anyone to go without shoes and thermal socks.

He hoped she'd be happy to go barefoot and then… He cut off that train of thought and turned the shower to cold.

Three freezing minutes later, with goosebumps on his goosebumps and a cock so shriveled he wondered if it would ever recover and come out to play, he switched the spray off and toweled himself briskly. What would he find in the bedroom?

He soon found the answer. Lindsey sprawled on the bed in some almost-there underwear, fast asleep. The lacy crop top and itty bitty thong left little to the imagination and conjured up some interesting scenarios. One swift glance and his cock showed it definitely hadn't lost the ability to call attention to itself and be ready to play.

That's one good thing then.

Michael took his time to enjoy the sight. She slumbered on, oblivious to his slow and thorough perusal. Did that make him a pervert? Whatever, she was his lady, he was determined about that. No matter they had split up before. That block to their relationship was long gone. After all, she might not be totally au fait with his new role at the moment but before many hours passed she would be.

He opened a drawer quietly and found clean boxers, t-shirt and jeans. If, as he rather supposed, he was going to spend more time up here, he'd need to increase his stash of clothes. Something Darke had said a few weeks earlier, about time to learn the intricacies of the Dispatchers' work on the island, made him suspect he was going to have to learn to drink whisky and like haggis.

Stereotypical thoughts. Enough already.

Quietly and unhurriedly Michael dressed, before he slid his feet into a pair of flip-flops and walked across to the bed, to shake Lindsey gently.

She jerked upright and only quick thinking on his part stopped her head and his from clashing. Michael pulled himself backwards and held onto her wrists before the fists she had formed met any part of his anatomy.

Lindsey blinked. "Wh…"

He kissed her nose and she wrinkled it. "Don't. It tickles."

"I like doing it." *And so I won't stop,* his tone inferred. "You fell asleep. Unless you want to go to the meeting like that, you better get some clothes on."

****

Oh god, oh god, trust me. Lindsey scrambled across the soft as anything mattress and tried to dispel the sleep from her foggy brain. She had only sat down to digest everything and get everything that had happened clear in her mind so she could report concisely to Darke.

After searching for footwear and only coming up with hiking socks and walking boots, she had flopped. Now she tugged a long sleeved t-shirt over her head and dragged on a pair of jeans that almost fit, if you discounted how many times she rolled them up at the hems. Someone was tall. Lindsey stood up and Michael smiled at her grimace as she glanced down to her ankles.

"Bought to fit anyone your size, be they five foot or six foot. Ready?"

"Shoes?" she asked. "I can't go around inside in those boots." She glared at the offending footwear. Clumpy, and no doubt great for clomping around the island. Not so good on the parquet floors she'd glimpsed. She'd bet they were a man's idea.

"Well, you could if you needed to," Michael said with an expression she distrusted. "But the general rule for our ladies is barefoot." He looked at her speculatively. "There's under floor heating."

Hmm, if he thinks that I'm his, he's got another thought coming. I'm not a ripe peach to fall into his lap. Well at least she hoped not. Not yet. They had a lot of talking to do first.

That tug of submission was getting bigger and more commanding by the minute and Lindsey did her best to shut it out. She needed time. Time to assimilate just what her emotions were *and* what she intended to do about it. Going barefoot was not on her immediate agenda.

"As I'm no one's lady, that doesn't apply." She ignored his knowing smile as she picked up the thick striped socks and pulled them over her bare feet, and also ignored his amused and knowing manner. "That'll do. I'm ready."

He laughed and shook his head in delight. "I'll let you think that for now."

Lindsey didn't bother to answer. He'd see soon enough. "Shall we?" She took the initiative and held out her hand. "Before someone comes to find us."

Michael considered her long enough for Lindsey to feel uncertain and then took her hand. "We better had." He opened the door and indicated the stairs. "Down and to the left. This part of the building is not for business."

Lindsey let him lead her to the lower floor and along a corridor painted in what she'd call institutional cream, until they came to a closed door. Michael dropped her hand and put his thumb on a bland dark grey square as he looked into the tiniest of mirrors. He glanced at her and smiled faintly. "Thumb print and face recognition. It had a hissy fit when Milo grew a moustache for Movember. It had to be reprogrammed to accept it. Now we all try not to change our appearance without warning someone." He pressed a series of numbers and then pressed one again. "That tells them you're with me and authorized to be. Double checked all the way."

The door opened smoothly, and he ushered Lindsey through the aperture and down some stairs. She shivered. The air was noticeably cooler here and her toes would be frozen without the socks. Well maybe not frozen but be mighty uncomfortable. Lindsey wished she had a jumper over the t-shirt she wore.

Michael noticed her movement and frowned. "It's usually warmer. But I've an inkling no one expected the visitors to be up here so fast. If it doesn't get any better, I'll find you something else to wear once we get to the conference room."

Thank goodness for that. Lindsey inclined her head and relished his hand at the back of her waist. She needed all the support she could get. The situation she'd found herself in was way out of her depth and she didn't enjoy the crawling sensation up her spine, which intimated something unpleasant was about to happen.

Michael stopped outside a bland, cream-painted door and went through the thumb, stare, and number routine again before he pushed the door open and ushered her inside the room.

"Michael, Lindsey." Darke, the sole occupant of the room, nodded at them as he leaned against a table and watched them as they advanced toward him. "Grab a seat and let's get started." He swung the nearest chair around and sat on it with his legs either side and his arms on the back. He waited until Michael held a chair out and Lindsey sat down. Once Michael followed suit, Darke gave each of them one long considering glance and then smiled. "First off, Lindsey you did well."

That made her jump. "I… er… only did what you told me to do."

Darke inclined his head in acknowledgement. "Exactly. You did what you were asked. No more, no less. Just what was needed. So many people can't accept that directives are just that. Telling you what is to be done. You did. That enabled Michael to do his job as well. Now he can hand over to Rio and Mac. They will find out who Dutt is killing for and why."

"I have no idea who," Lindsey said. "But I'd bet it's because he wants, well, needs, money. He tried to tap me up for a grand once and I told him no way was I in a position to lend money. And he often did a hurried 'no we'll go this way' when he saw someone in the distance, and we had to backtrack. So, I reckon he owes money and well, he hasn't got it."

Darke pursed his lips. "It falls in with things we've learned."

"And it makes a lot of sense to the sort of stuff he had me doing," Michael added. "Lots of seemingly innocent deliveries but to strange places."

"Those innocent deliveries made up around three quarters of what you did," Darke said. "It was the fourth quarter that was money laundering."

"Figures then. He was abroad and then he wasn't," Lindsey said. "I guess it got a bit too hot in sunny Spain. In more ways than one."

"You could say that. His… er… ex lady friend at the time was very fond of pillow talk. He is, or I should say was, excellent at extracting information from unsuspecting ladies. That however, was a year or so ago. Much to my operative's delight. It made his job all the more easier." Darke smiled sardonically. "He was considerably better at it. Sadly it has all changed, but we got what we needed."

Now she was intrigued, but knew it wasn't the time to ask those sorts of questions. She shuddered. Darke saw and fetched a pair of Uggs and a thick cardigan from a cupboard and handed them to her. "Until you become acclimatized to going barefoot."

She didn't think she'd better argue, and after all she wanted the garments. Lindsey murmured her thanks and began to pull the overlarge boyfriend cardi around her without bothering to thread her arms though the sleeves. That first and Uggs next. They looked a bit snug and she might need to remove the socks to get them on.

"Plus," Darke continued in that same flat, faintly menacing tone, "a certain gang we've been chasing to tie in with money laundering seems to be losing rivals at a rate of knots. Amos managed to infiltrate one of them, and discovered what was happening to its operatives. All people working to undermine our stability, which means in one way they are no loss. Sadly, though, it happens only to strengthen the group who are working the hardest to upset the lives of the British people. Their jobs, their homes, their ideals. And I'm not willing to let that happen. But nor can I condone what is happening and where those bodies are ending up."

"As the latest whisky bottle?" Michael said with an upward inflection.

"Exactly. Therefore." Darke got up and began to prowl around the room. "I need you to both write up your reports and once we have the results of Dutt's questioning we will know how to proceed. Meanwhile, I've asked Rio to pop in and add his two penn'orth. He'll be with you to do the questioning, Michael. Lindsey, it will give you a chance to catch up on your much-needed sleep. And meet our ladies who will be able to reassure you that actually we are all incredibly normal."

That sounded perfect. She grinned, wondered who Amos was, and hid yet another yawn as there was a knock on the door. The thought of sleep was ever more alluring. Lindsey swung around to see who this Rio was.

Stared and stood up.

"You fucking bastard."

He had to duck in a hurry to avoid first one and then another leather Ugg boot as they missed his head by inches.

"What the—"

Darke smirked. "Be thankful it's only boots. She got ninety-nine percent in both knife throwing and target practice."

Chapter Eight

Michael raced across the room and grabbed Lindsey around her waist as Rio took one menacing step toward her, shook his head in annoyance and instead picked up the boots and put them neatly side by side next to the doorjamb. Well away, Michael noted, from his lady.

"What, pet, is that all about?" Michael asked as he dodged her flailing legs and feet and carried her back to where Darke stood. He held her firmly, with her legs trapped between his thighs, and her arms imprisoned inside his. Then he stared at Darke. The expression on his boss's face told him a lot.

"You bloody didn't."

Darke shrugged. "It was standard procedure. We need to be sure our operatives do not indulge in sharing secrets over sex. At that time Rio was the one to do it. Now, well… now it's not him."

"Andie wouldn't stand for it," Rio said. "And to be honest now, nor would I. Then it was different. I was footloose and fancy free." He looked bleak. "It was crap and shite, but I did my job and was good at it. Andie wasn't mine then."

"Nor was I, you asshole, and it was me you tried to seduce. Well at least you didn't get into my knickers. Your technique must have been slipping." Lindsey sounded fit to burst. "Poor woman, this Andie. You know, with hindsight I feel sorry for *any* woman involved with *any* of you. 'My woman,'" she mimicked. "Any woman with anything about her is her own self. Not a chattel. God you all make me sick. Why did I think I would fit in here? Not a fucking chance. I'm out of it. I quit."

"Pet." Michael kept his voice flat and

unthreatening, but he hoped with enough of the Dom in it to get through her rage. "No more. These things happened for a reason. You had to be tested. When you calm down you will see that."

If he thought that might ease her temper, he was way off the mark. She just stared at him scathingly. "Bollocks. Lothario there tried it on. Did his best to fuck me and fool me. Well poor him. His cock couldn't manage and nor could his quest— *oopft Mnighph!*" Michael held her firm as Rio gagged her with swift efficiency. That, he reckoned, had killed any chance of their happy ever after happening.

"Enough, pet. You can quit later. First we need to write our reports." She glared at him and shook her head vehemently.

"Oh, yes, believe me you will. Even if I tie you down to do it." He waited until she dropped her icy gaze and then went on. "You, pet, are a professional. You did a good job. Whether you stay or go, you owe it to yourself to finish what you started. Yes?" He waited for her infinitesimal nod. "Good girl. If I take your gag off do you give me your word you won't rip up again?" This time it was several seconds longer before she nodded.

Thank the lord for that. As he picked at Rio's knot—it was far too complicated for a simple gag—he intercepted an amused glance between Rio and Darke and scowled. If Lindsey saw that, they would be back where they started.

Thankfully she didn't, or if she did, chose not to comment. Darke handed her a bottle of water as the cloth left her face and she took it with a word of thanks, before she drank deeply.

"Where do I go to write this load of...." Michael gave her a warning look and she stopped speaking abruptly. "This information you need," she finished. "The sooner I get it done the better."

"I agree." Darke indicated a door to his left. "In there. You'll find all you need. Michael will accompany you in a moment." His voice left no room for argument.

Michael watched as Lindsey's expression changed and for one moment he wondered if her rage would get the better of her, and she would argue. He could imagine her difficulty. Then she stood. "Thank you." Without a further look at any of them she walked, very dignified, across the room and disappeared from view. The door closed with a very controlled thud.

Michael winced as he went to follow her. Darke stopped him with one hand in the air. "One minute."

For the count of five no one moved, then Darke waved both Michael and Rio to the desk. Once all three were seated Darke looked from one to the other. "Well that went particularly badly," he remarked as he steepled his chin on his fingertips. "Not my finest moment I admit."

"Nor was not mentioning her aim," Rio said. "Why only ninety-nine?"

Darke wore his most enigmatic expression. "No one's perfect. You need something to strive for. And I didn't want to put you on your guard, so telling you how good she was at self-defense would have been counterproductive. Do you think she'll go?" he asked Michael. "I hope not; we could do with her here with you. With the others either expecting or new mothers I need a female's view on things. Nothing against our ladies but they are a bit preoccupied these days."

"Andie?" Michael asked as Rio smirked and nodded. "Bloody hell, mate, you're a fast worker. We'll have to rename this place Fertility Isle at this rate."

"We're not getting any younger but for fuck's sake don't tell her I said that." Rio stretched his long legs out in front of him. "She's paranoid enough about being an aged prima gravida or sommat as it is. Oh, and for the record, your lady was not at all interested in me, or giving away any secrets about anything. I didn't even know she was your ex 'til Darke told me after. She was as tight-lipped as, well, as whatever you chose."

"Just what we need in an operative," Darke said. "Anyway, that's for later. Let's get the plan of action."

****

"Bloody, sodding, crappy, moronic, ah shit." Lindsey moved away from the laptop she'd been working on. It was that or smash her fist into the screen and go into a full-blown rage. She sniffed and swore again instead. Wet keys were not the way to go and her tears were beginning to blind her. Not that she had fancied Rio, anything but. He might look like sex on legs but it did nothing for her. Neither then or now. However, that wasn't the point. She felt betrayed by all she believed in and it hurt. Not just the fact that Darke had tested her in such a way, but that Michael had accepted it was something they did. How would he have felt, she wondered if Rio, who she'd known as Don, had reported 'hey we fucked like rabbits' and she'd also compared him favorably to the way Michael screwed?

"I'd have killed him the way we kill traitors," Michael said quietly as he walked soft-footed across the room. "Fed him alive to the pigs. Then spent days showing you just how wrong you were. You know, pet, you need to stop that tendency of talking out loud. Especially when questioning someone's virility."

She jumped and wiped her eyes impatiently. "I never used to. Just these last few days and only it seems when you're around. God I hate this stupid attitude, but that is how I feel. Daft, stupid and used." She kicked the desk leg and winced. "Shit."

"Pet," he used the sobriquet on purpose. "You are none of those, so stop that now. Rio was damned good at that part of his job. He could charm the knickers off anyone, except, it seems, you. So yes, you are bloody good. Stop doubting yourself, get your side of the thing down in a document and send it to Darke. Then we can move forward."

"Hmm. What about you?" She tapped her fingers on the desk, no longer sure what moving forward meant. Why did he look so complacent? "Don't you have to do a report as well?"

Michael grinned. "I've done it verbally. I'm off to interrogate Dutt."

Lindsey blew her nose on the wad of tissues she'd found in the desk drawer. "I want to come," she said in a firm voice as she eyeballed him with such a fierce expression he winced. "He fucked around with me more than once. I want to hear what he says. Don't say no. I'll stop the other side of the mirror or whatever Darke and whoever else hide behind, but I need to be in on the denouement. Can't you see?" She appealed to him. "I need closure."

Michael inclined his head. "I guessed as much and so did Darke. He also said you had a good eye for anomalies. Yeah, you can be an observer."

He chuckled as she high-fived. "Come on then, what are we waiting for?" Lindsey scrambled to her feet.

Michael looked at her sock clad feet. "Put your boots on and the cardigan, properly. It's not as cozy in the interrogation wing."

She shivered. This was real. Not a book or a film where the actors went home to their wives and comfy lifestyles. Where every time someone said 'cut' they got hot water bottles or a mug of coffee. This was real, nasty espionage and if someone said 'cut' there could well be loss of blood—or a limb. Whatever you thought about that, or the way potential or real traitors were dealt with, betraying your country was not acceptable. Lindsey pulled on the boots Michael handed her, glad to see they fit over the socks and she wouldn't have to do without that layer, and then added the long cashmere cardigan. She immediately felt ten degrees warmer. "Ready."

"Then come with me. Remember you're not there to get your kicks if he starts to blubber like a baby. Or comment on the techniques used. I warn you now they can be harsh. Very harsh, and if you think you're gonna toss your cookies go into the bathroom and don't distract Darke and whoever else is there. Take note or notes. You're there to recognize anything that seems out of order. Yes?"

Lindsey nodded, and hoped her stomach would stop churning. She never did get that steak and chips, and hunger, combined with whatever emotion she had, was not a good combination. On cue her tummy rumbled.

"Here." Michael handed her a protein bar. "Coffee will be in the room. Okay?"

"Yes. Thanks." She, unwrapped it, took a healthy bite and pocketed the wrapper. Try as she might she couldn't stop her pulse racing. This man was everything she needed and wanted. How could she have been so dumb as to walk off as she did? Why didn't she have the ability to trust? How could she have thrown away the chance to discover all they could be?

It was different then. And I didn't believe someone like him really loved someone like me. She didn't intend to make the same mistakes again. Now it was time to talk and listen, to consider and be together again? Lordy, she hoped so. "Yes," she said again firmly once her mouth was empty. "I know what to do and how to do it."

"Excellent." Michael took a firm grip on the

untidy plait that swung over one shoulder and tugged on it until she took two steps toward him and they touched. His cock was a hard rod against her stomach. Lindsey went on tiptoe and pressed closer. His breath was warm on her neck, his breathing choppy and yes, she was certain his dick swelled, and nudged her.

Michael groaned and she echoed it. "Minx," he said in an agonized voice. "We've no time for this at the moment." Even so, he slid his hand up under her t-shirt and bra and pinched one nipple firmly.

It seemed impossible for it to harden further but she swore it did and the pleasure-pain hit her with such force she moaned and swayed. "More." Was that thready voice really hers?

It seemed so.

"Later, my pet. Later, all this and more will be yours." He put her hand on his cock and squeezed her fingers around it before he removed her digits, and took a step back. "Remember you're mine. No coming until I say so. No rubbing yourself, no trying to get yourself off and no, but no, pinching, tweaking, or fingers inside you. You understand?"

"Wha… eh?" Lindsey heard his words as if they were through a curtain. The smack to her pussy mound made her jump. "What?"

"No coming. Now is for work, later is for talk and play."

She pouted. Just when she'd made her mind up to see what they still had between them, he demanded such a hard thing to do.

Michael's quiet but firm words penetrated her aroused mind. "We have all the time we need for us once we finish the job. Now will you do as I say?"

He might not have uttered the words 'as your Sir demands' but it was implicit.

Now or never. Lindsey didn't hesitate. "Yes, Sir."
His smile was worth everything she desired.

Chapter Nine

Michael rubbed his gritty eyes and bit back a yawn. God, he was knackered. How long since he had slept?

Too bloody long.

Not long enough, though, not to understand the guy in front of them was sweating buckets, as guilty as hell, and trying desperately to find a scapegoat for his actions.

Beside Michael, Mac stood, arms folded, and stared impassively at the sobbing broken man, half curled up in a ball in front of them. They hadn't laid a finger on him. He'd taken one look at them and his surroundings, and passed out. When they revived him —"not that I want the bugger to live, but he's not cheating the pigs out of a meal"— he'd morphed into the mess they could see.

"So, it wasn't your fault, any of it," Michael mimicked, as Mac kicked Dutt none too gently in the balls with one toe-capped foot. Not hard enough to cause proper injury, just enough to show they meant business. It was the first time Dutt had been touched, other than to bring him into the room and manacle him to the chair. Intimidation had been enough. Those manacles were the only things that had stopped him slumping to the floor. "You're a bloody wuss."

"Do…don't touch me…"

"Shit, now he's begging." Michael did the exaggerated eyes to the ceiling action that worked so effectively. "We haven't touched you—yet. But I will if you don't man up. You deserve it for what you did to my lady. And to Roddy Archer's better half. Now, I might be magnanimous. Roddy-boy won't. "

"Your lady?" Dutt looked around wildly and

shook his head. He sniffled and gulped back some snotty snivel. "Fuck no… Stella? She was… I didn't… It was… Not my fault."

"Someone forced you to fuck her eh? To screw her and use her."

Dutt groaned. "She wanted it."

"And her not so better prisoner other half was none too pleased when he heard. Now I wonder why that was eh? It couldn't be because she was using his money to feather her nest, and while he accepted that, he was damned if he'd pay to keep you in the lap of luxury as well. Shagging his woman was acceptable, drinking his finest single malt was not."

"I was stitched up," Dutt moaned. "It wasn't my fault."

"Load of crap," Mac said. "Bullshit. You did the sewing, mate, no one else."

Dutt glowered, sullenly. "I had to. Either I disposed of his bodies for him or he disposed of me."

"Who?"

Dutt shook his head and firmed his lips. "He'd kill me if I say anything."

"Pity he hasn't already, it would have saved us a job," Michael said casually. "Who are we talking about?"

Dutt swallowed. "Come on Coultery, you helped me. You're in it as deep as I am."

"Wrong. Ah, I'll leave him to you." Michael said to Mac as Milo entered the room. "After all, Roddy Archer might be grateful we've sorted out his problem. Sadly he won't be able to launder, or make body glass for a bit, but hey that's life."

"You knew? You fucker! You know and you've been stringing me along. You…" Dutt howled and strained against his restraints. "You're as guilty as me. You drove the van. You knew. You were one of us."

"Nope. I was and still am a Dispatcher. I'm employed to get rid of vermin like you. Now, I've got to see a lady about an attitude."

Milo grunted. "Good luck. I'll be betting we both have a similar conversation later. Tonight was supposed to be cinema night. The ladies were looking forward to it. They watch the film, we suffer it, and provide the goodies."

"Yeah? What were you going to watch?"

Milo rolled his eyes. "*Mamma Mia*."

Michael bit back a grin. "At least it's not a so-called true life spy story."

"Yeah," Milo agreed. "There is that." He contemplated Dutt. "No one would believe us if we put the record straight. I mean feed a traitor alive to the pigs? Unbelievable."

Dutt went ashen.

Milo laughed. "They're ready for dinner. Come on you."

"Noooooo."

Michael heard Dutt's screams as he walked out of the room and shut the door behind him.

Let Mac and Milo do the necessary, he had a lady to see and a life to sort out. He popped his head into the room where Darke still watched the proceedings next door.

"Just left. I didn't think there was much point in making her watch the next bit. Not that. Not until you both decide what you're going to do. Together or apart."

"Thanks for that. And when we know I'll make sure you do." Whistling, Michael turned on his heels and headed for the stairs, took them two at a time and mentally shed his work persona as he entered his apartment. He didn't need to take more than three steps to know it was empty.

No Lindsey.

Even though he was certain the rooms had no occupant, Michael walked through each room in turn, just to make certain his senses hadn't let him down.

They hadn't.

Where the hell was she? She couldn't have gone far, he accepted that. But the sensation of hurt, that she wasn't there waiting for him, hit him hard.

Think, don't sulk. Where in this building is she likely to be?

Film night. What was the betting one of their ladies had discovered Lindsey was around and on her own and persuaded her to join them?

He wouldn't bet against that.

The sense of relief that Lindsey would be with Astrid, Kirsten, Emma and Andie was overwhelming. He wondered briefly if he should be worried, because those ladies together were a formidable force to be reckoned with. However, if he and Lindsey stayed together, and as Darke intimated he'd be based here on Dark Isle—or as it was also known, Death Isle, both apt names—it would be inevitable she'd join forces with the other women.

However he could do without them giving her any ammunition, couched as advice, on how to go forward.

Michael headed for the shower to get rid of the crawling sensation Dutt had given him. Within three minutes, after one of the shortest showers on record, he dressed in a clean black t-shirt, and chuckled to himself at how stereotypical he was. Black T, jeans or leather trousers. Once a Dom, always a Dom. Okay it wasn't a uniform per se, but he knew he and the others on the Island always seemed to dress similarly when they wanted to be in charge. Which, as they were all dominant characters, was most of the time.

Not that it bothered him to wear colors. His

favorite shirt was a pale green-blue.

The color of Lindsey's eyes.

That had never struck him before. Michael inwardly mocked himself for his foibles as he went into the kitchen to get a glass of juice before he headed for the cozy room used as a cinema. Interviewing, interrogating, torture, call it what you will, not only made him feel grubby, it dehydrated him as well.

The note was written in bright pink ink and stuck to the fridge door.

—'Willingly kidnapped. Bring wine and chocolate to arrange my release. P.S. after 10 pm'—

It was signed with five smiley faces and a curly letter L.

Michel grinned as he retrieved the bottle of juice, went to drink, remembered he had a guest and poured the liquid into a glass instead of gulping it from the bottle. Then he found a multi pack of mini bars he didn't know he had—Astrid he surmised, she was the oldest and the supposed the leader of the ladies—chose a bottle of wine he did know about, a bottle of sparkling non alcoholic grape juice he'd never seen before—no doubt Astrid again—and headed out.

He heard the cacophony well before he reached the source.

Several inharmonic voices singing, shouting, caterwauling, murdering 'Does Your Mother Know'. No one had mentioned it was the sing-a-long—screech along—version of the film.

There was a second of blessed silence as he approached the door and then hysterical giggling.

Dare he knock? Michael took a deep breath, checked his watch and settled to wait.

****

Astrid turned the bottle she held upside down.

"All gone. No more grape juice."

Emma scowled at the bottle *she* held. "Nor wine. And as I've just stopped feeding I can have wine. Damn. Any chocolate?"

"Nope. Not even a coffee cream." Kirsten waved an empty box. "What time is it?"

Lindsey glanced at the clock on the wall. "Two minutes to ten."

"Hmm… well, knowing the Dispatchers, I betcha if Michael has had time to see your—our—note, he'll knock dead on time. Then, my dear, you're on your own. If you want to be." Andie cocked her head. "If not, we'll be on your side."

Lindsey looked from one to other of her new friends and smiled gratefully. They had livened up her evening, given her support and advice and, she accepted, would run interference if needed. Even if it got them into trouble with their Sirs and Masters. For each had admitted their relationships with their menfolk, given her an insight into living with a Dom who was also a Dispatcher, and how they coped living on an island in the middle of a loch.

It all sounded perfect. But would she have the chance to experience it?

The clock whirred as the hands moved. The knock on the door made each one of them jump.

Astrid smiled at Lindsey. "Over to you."

Lindsey scrambled to her feet as another, more impatient rap tattooed on the wooden door. "Yeah. Wish me luck, and hopefully I'll see you all soon. If I don't, well, thank you."

"Luck, not that you'll need it."

"You will. See us. Betcha."

"Go slay him, or whatever."

Andie grinned at Lindsey. "Just enjoy."

Lindsey accepted their flurry of kisses and advice, and walked unhurriedly to the door. It was the only way she could stop her knees knocking. Behind her the soundtrack of the film started to play, 'I Have a Dream'. So did she.

Michael—drop dead gorgeous, dressed to perfection and with the sort of demeanor that was panty-wetting, submission-making, and just what she yearned for—leaned on the doorjamb and waved a carrier. "Provisions as requested. Where do you want them?"

"I'll take them, thanks, goodbye, be good both of you, and be careful." Astrid whisked the bag out of Michael's hands and disappeared again.

Lindsey drank in the sight of him. Just to see him standing there, clothed as he was, brought every iota of her submissive nature to the fore. She swallowed and fought not to dip her head or lower her eyes. She might want to sub to him, but, and it was a big but, could she? What was going to be their future if she did, or indeed did not? That had to be decided first.

"Will you come with me?" Michael's tone was, she was certain, deliberately neutral. "Either to the apartment or to another room where we can be alone."

The only thing that made her understand he was as nervous as she was the erratic pulse that showed briefly in his neck.

"Of course." She was proud of her steady voice. "To wherever you prefer." What would he decide?

To Lindsey's amazement, Michael chuckled. "I'd prefer the room, and I'm taking you to the apartment." He paused. "First." He held out his hand and Lindsey grasped it. "Did you enjoy yourself with the girls?" he asked as they retraced their steps to the apartment. "They weren't too overwhelming?"

"They were great. Gave me so much

information." Lindsey gave a little skip. "Really helpful."

Michael grimaced. "I was afraid of that." He ushered her inside his apartment and closed and locked the door behind them. "I'm convinced Emma has housebreaking tendencies. This discussion and whatever else follows is for us alone. No eavesdroppers, cheerleaders, or voyeurs. Yes?"

"Oh yes." It was going to be difficult enough as it was, without extraneous advice. Lindsey took a deep breath, sat on the settee and waited as Michael leaned against the fireplace and contemplated her. Dare she go first? Get her opinion and her intentions known?

Why not? She had nothing to lose.

"You know, I wondered if I would ever get the chance to say this," she began as Michael straightened, took three steps across the room, and sat backward on a ladder-back chair in front of her. "What is it with men sitting like that?" she began and then shook her head. "No, don't answer that, it'll make me forget what I want to say. Okay?"

Michael inclined his head. "Say away."

Phew.

"I was a fool," she said frankly as she twisted her hands together to stop them shaking. This could determine the rest of her life. "I know you didn't exactly give me much to go on or to trust you with, but I should have been patient, held my wheesht as I've heard it said and not got mardy."

"You had good reason to be angry," Michael said wryly. "I wasn't forthcoming. Okay I wasn't able to be, but really I should have just changed departments. You were worth it. I was too bloody stubborn."

"We both were," Lindsey said quietly. This was it. She mentally 'girded her loins', ignored the erratic beat of her heart and took a deep breath. Now or never.

"Sadly, I can't turn back time, but I can ask, Sir, please can we have another chance?"

It was so very hard not to squirm under his intense scrutiny. What was he thinking?

She'd counted to twenty under her breath before he stood up and slowly tugged her hair. "Stand up."

No please, no politeness, but the look in his eyes had her scrambling to her feet. "Sir?" The title seemed both natural and needed.

"Really, pet?" Michael gripped her chin. "Is that because you think I want to hear it or because you need it and want it?"

"I hope you want to hear it, Sir," she said, honestly. "But I need it." She worried her lip and his tap on her pussy made her stop immediately. "Sorry, Sir. It's hard to put it into words, but it wasn't until I saw you again I realized what I'd denied myself. Denied us. The chance to be what we are—or I think we are—supposed to be. Dom and sub. My Dom and your sub." Her voice trailed off. She didn't want to come across as pushy or needy even if she knew at that moment it would be easy to be both. "I just think we deserve another chance."

"And if I say no? What then?"

That was not the easiest question in the world to answer.

Chapter Ten

Michael studied his wan-faced pet, and waited not so patiently for her to answer him. Oh, he had no intention of letting her go. Dom and sub they would be once more, *and* before they met up with anyone else again, and she heard what Darke had in mind for her.

"Well?" he asked as the silence lengthened. "Cat got your tongue or can't you answer?"

She glared. She had a good line in glares. "I would do my damnedest to change your mind, *Sir*."

"Fair enough." He'd ignore the sass for now. This was a tricky time for both of them. Negotiations were going to have to be navigated before long. But first. "Vanilla or a little scene? Your choice."

In answer she slid to her knees, dipped her head and put her hands behind her back. It was gratifying to see how she scrambled to present herself. Always she had done it when he asked but admitted she felt silly. To see her behave in that way without him asking was cum-inducing to say the least.

The crunch would come when, as he intended to, he pushed her out of her comfort zone. Tried her with things she'd always hesitated over before. Not hard limits but definitely things she'd put as 'maybe one day' when they had discussed them.

Michael waited until Lindsey was on her knees in front of him and hunkered down, to lift her chin up so she looked him in the eyes. "Do you remember your safe words? If so, repeat them now. There will be no mistakes here, pet. This is how we need to go on."

"Yes Sir, Red is stop now. We may discuss whatever later but for now it is an immediate halt, not to be repeated until we have talked about it. Yellow, stop

and we can discuss it now, and green go ahead, it is fine."
Her voice rang out with trust and confidence and
Michael's heart gave a happy lurch to hear it.

"And you know we will be negotiating from
scratch? We are not who we were all those years ago.
This is the new us."

"I understand that." Lindsey nodded emphatically.
"I'm no longer the person who didn't trust you or even
try to understand what you had to cope with."

"Good, and I'm not the man who wasn't prepared
to try and meet you half way, pet," Michael assured her.
"We were both in the wrong. Hopefully we can now
forget the Lindsey and Michael of those days and
concentrate on the Lindsey and Michael of now. Yes?"

"Oh yes."

"Then remember your safe words." He stood up
and with slow deliberate movements, flicked open the
snap on his jeans, lowered the zipper, and let his
engorged and rock hard cock out of the denim confines.
"Are you ready to play a little?"

She nodded.

"Vocalize," Michael said patiently. "I'm not a
mind reader all of the time."

"Shoot, I forgot. Yes Sir."

Michael chuckled. "We both have a lot to
remember. Do you want to go over your limits now, or do
we see how things go? I promise to ask before I do
anything at all. As long as you promise to be up front and
honest. For instance…"

Lindsey's eyes widened as he slowly and
deliberately stroked the length, gathered his pre cum onto
his finger and held his hand out.

"Lick it pet, or safe word."

Her eyes widened but she delicately swiped her
tongue over his shining digit "That, Sir is green."

"Nice now, safe word or suck me off." He waited as she gulped and hesitated. She swayed towards him and straightened. Many people didn't involve sex in their play; he and Lindsey always had and that was how he wanted it to be now. However, he remembered oral was something she'd never been keen on and eventually said it was a soft limit. It had never changed and nor had she gone down on him more than a few times, and never ever swallowed his cum. Not something he'd ever encountered before or indeed after Lindsey. She'd tried and after gagging and throwing up, had said swallowing was a big fat red no-no. He'd accepted it, but had missed that special closeness only being jerked off by your partner could bring. But Lindsey was his lady, his sub, he had loved her—still did—and her pleasure came first.

Perhaps it was unfair to throw her into this scenario so quickly, but he knew his pet. She could go round the houses forever. He intended to show her he would not be fazed or upset by her limits whatever.

"Pet, you need to tell me where you are in this. Safe word." He rapped his demands out. "Now."

"Green to lick," she said so softly he had to strain to hear. "I hope." She took his cock in between her hands and delicately licked the head.

His pre-cum leaked fast and furious and she drew back and looked at it.

Typical. The one time I could do with it taking its time, it comes like the clappers.

"It's fine," she said with awe in her voice. "Green." She took more of his length in her mouth and began to nibble and suck.

He saw stars as the tug and pull became stronger. God almighty did she *know* the affect she was having on him? He was going to come if she didn't slow down or pull back.

"Pet, enough, I'm about to shoot." Michael tugged her hair, hard enough to make her release him. Or so he hoped.

"Lindsey. Pet, stop now." Did he sound Dom-like enough? It was bloody hard when half of him would like no more than to fuck her mouth until he filled it with cum, and watched the excess run down her cheeks. But he didn't truly want to. Not yet. Baby steps.

His command evidently got to her because she moved her mouth from his cock with a gentle plop. The confusion and hurt in her eyes hit him. "Pet, baby steps," he said softly as he helped her to her feet. "I would happily fill your mouth and fuck it. But, not today. We have so much more to explore and hopefully have a lifetime to do everything in." Would she understand without him getting too graphic? "I want to fuck your sweet pussy. Fill you that way. Relearn how you sigh and how well our bodies mesh. Make you scream as you come. Shudder and shake for me. Show you how much I love you, have never stopped loving you, and want this to be our happy ever after."

Lindsey sighed and her eyes became misty. "Sir, My Michael, oh yes. I feel the same. You are mine. My lover, my friend and my Sir. I want it all as well."

"First then." Michael paused, tugged off her cardigan and threw it onto the floor. That's better. Now…" He unzipped her jeans so he could run one finger around her panty leg. "Firstly, I want you naked so I can spank your sweet ass until it's the rosy color of that cushion over there." He slid her panties and jeans down her legs and helped her step out of them. "I want to see my handprint and know that outline shows you are mine. Arms up." Her t-shirt followed the cardigan. "Stand still, just like that with your arms up. Don't lower them."

Michael waited as she did as he demanded,

grabbed her ass hard to keep her in place and lowered his lips to the lacy cups of her bra.

And sucked hard.

Lindsey bucked. "Oh grief oh my, oh hell…Oh god, Green bloody green."

He took that as a good sign, let go of her nipples and ignored her moan as he blew on each hard nub in turn. Deftly he unclipped her bra and flung it in the direction of the rest of her clothes. Now he wished he'd taken her to the playroom. He knew no one was playing in it and he had a cupboard full of delicious things he could use on her. All still new and in their packets. Here, he'd have to be innovative and make do.

At least he had his hands. Michael unclenched his fingers and watched her pupils dilate as he smacked her ass a couple of times. "What color are clothes pegs?" he asked casually. "Specifically on your breasts, nipples and ass."

"Clo… Pegs?" Her voice rose to a high-pitched squeak. "Pegs on my…oh my…" She blinked. "Can you?"

Michael smiled. "Oh yes. But maybe not yet?"

She nodded. "Perhaps not. I need to rediscover pain, I reckon. Let's say yellow."

"Then maybe we should start." He pondered for a moment. "Here, I think." He sat on the nearest chair and pulled her to lie over his lap, head to one side, legs to the other. "Color, pet?"

He could visualize her rolling her eyes at him for being so insistent. However she answered him readily, and politely. "Green, Sir."

"Then, pet, count. Ten on each side and then I'm going to fuck your wet and willing pussy."

"Yes, *Sir,*" she said fervently.

Michael laughed as he raised his hand. He hit her

right buttock firmly and then rubbed away the sting as she gasped.

"O…One."

"Good girl." He repeated the actions on the other globe. By six on each side Lindsey was writhing and he opened his legs enough to reach between them and pinch her clit hard. "No coming or I'll stop now."

"Eh?" She sounded dazed. "F…flip, no…no. Don't stop."

"Then behave." He held his hand aloft just long enough, he decided, for her to wonder if he intended to continue, and then recommenced his smacks.

They were both breathing heavily when he lifted her, carried her to the bed and carefully set her down on her stomach. His handprints glowed satisfactorily on each ass cheek. "One day I must take a picture of that," he mused as he arranged her on her knees with a pillow under her stomach, her head cradled on her arms and her ass high and ready for him. Next time he'd fuck her there, he promised himself. Strangely that hadn't been a limit.

Not now though. "Now, I'm going to fuck your pussy and wait for you to scream your completion. Give me your climax, pet, I'm waiting for it." He pushed his cock into her with little finesse. He'd felt her juices on his legs as he spanked her and knew—hoped to hell—she was ready for him.

He was correct. Lindsey lifted her ass high to accommodate him and joined his thrust and retreat with a fervor that astounded him.

"I want it all," she chanted breathlessly. "I want everything you give me. I want you…ooo argh fuck it… I'm…gonna…"

"Come now." He pinched one swaying tit and held onto it hard. Felt her convulse around him and let himself go. Hot cum flooded out of him and into her. He thrust rapidly, determined to last as long as he could. Their shouts and groans mingled until, goodness knows how long later, still breathing heavily, they quieted. Eventually, his cock slid out of her and he rolled onto his back to cradle her on top of him.

"I love you. I never stopped," he said quietly as he stroked her hair. "You are my world. Without you in it the light is dark, the days long and unfulfilled, and the future bleak."

She lifted her head so her greeny-blue eyes stared at him seriously. "Good, because now I know why no one ever got past first base with me. I was committed to you. Bound to my Sir." She pressed a kiss to his chest and wrinkled her nose. "Chest hair. It tickles."

He laughed. "You can shave it sometime. Not now though. So we are a couple? Partners? Dom and Sub? And maybe one day again husband and wife. Will you, when the time is right, wear my ring? Wear my collar? What do you say, my pet?"

"As my Sir says." She grinned widely and flung her arms around his neck. "All of the aforementioned, please, Sir. Oh God, I want you with me forever. I want you in me. I want you every which way. And Sir, I want to feel the sweet pleasure pain only you can give me. Forever. I want it all, but only with you."

The End

KERA FAIRE

EVERNIGHT PUBLISHING ®

www.evernightpublishing.com